The Blue Germ

Maurice Nicoll

The Blue Germ

ISBN: 978-1-64799-360-3

CONTENTS

CHAPTER I

BLACK MAGIC

I had just finished breakfast, and deeply perplexed had risen from the table in order to get a box of matches to light a cigarette, when my black cat got between my feet and tripped me up.

I fell forwards, making a clutch at the table-cloth. My forehead struck the corner of the fender and the last thing I remembered was a crash of falling crockery. Then all became darkness. My parlour-maid found me lying face downwards on the hearth-rug ten minutes later. My cat was sitting near my head, blinking contentedly at the fire. A little blood was oozing from a wound above my left eye.

They carried me up to my bedroom and sent for my colleague, Wilfred Hammer, who lived next door. For three days I lay insensible, and Hammer came in continually, whenever he could spare the time from his patients, and brooded over me. On the fourth day I began to move about in my bed, restless and muttering, and Hammer told me afterwards that I seemed to be talking of a black cat. On the night of the fourth day I suddenly opened my eyes. My perplexity had left me. An idea, clear as crystal, was now in my mind.

From that moment my confinement to bed was a source of impatience to me. Hammer, large, fair, square-headed, and imperturbable, insisted on complete rest, and I chafed under the restraint. I had only one desire—to get up, slip down to St. Dane's Hospital in my car, mount the bare stone steps that led up to the laboratory and begin work at once.

"Let me up, Hammer," I implored.

"My dear fellow, you're semi-delirious."

"I must get up," I muttered.

He laughed slowly.

"Not for another week or two, Harden. How is the black cat?"

"That cat is a wizard."

I lay watching him between half-closed eyelids.

"He gave me the idea."

"He gave you a nasty concussion," said Hammer.

"It was probably the only way to the idea," I answered. "I tell you the cat is a wizard. He did it on purpose. He's a black magician."

1

Hammer laughed again, and went towards the door.

"Then the idea must be black magic," he said.

I smiled painfully, for my head was throbbing. But I was happier then than I had ever been, for I had solved the problem that had haunted my brain for ten years.

"There's no such thing as black magic," I said.

Three weeks later I beheld the miracle. It was wrought on the last day of December, in the laboratory of the hospital, high above the gloom and squalor of the city. The miracle occurred within a brilliant little circle of light, and I saw it with my eye glued to a microscope. It passed off swiftly and quietly, and though I expected it, I was filled with a great wonder and amazement.

To a lay mind the amazement with which I beheld the miracle will require explanation. I had witnessed the transformation of one germ into another; a thing which is similar to a man seeing a flock of sheep on a hill-side change suddenly into a herd of cattle. For many minutes I continued to move the slide in an aimless way with trembling fingers. My temperament is earthy; it had once occurred to me quite seriously that if I saw a miracle I would probably go mad under the strain. Now that I had seen one, after the first flash of realization my mind was listless and dull, and all feeling of surprise had died away. The black rods floated with slow motion in the minute currents of fluid I had introduced. The faint roar of London came up from far below; the clock ticked steadily and the microscope lamp shone with silent radiance. And I, Richard Harden, sat dangling my short legs on the high stool, thinking and thinking....

That night I wrote to Professor Sarakoff. A month later I was on my way to Russia.

CHAPTER II

SARAKOFF'S MANIFESTO

The recollection of my meeting with Sarakoff remains vividly in my mind. I was shown into a large bare room, heated by an immense stove like an iron pagoda. The floor was of light yellow polished wood; the walls were white-washed, and covered with pencil marks. A big table covered with papers and books stood at one end. At the other, through an open doorway, there was a glimpse of a laboratory. Sarakoff stood in the centre of the room, his hands deep in his pockets, his pipe sending up clouds of smoke, his tall muscular frame tilted back. His eyes were fixed on an extraordinary object that crawled slowly over the polished floor. It was a gigantic tortoise—a specimen of Testudo elephantopus—a huge cumbersome brute. Its ancient, scaly head was thrust out and its eyes gleamed with a kind of sharp intelligence. The surface of its vast and massive shell was covered over with scribbles in white chalk—notes made by Sarakoff who was in the habit of jotting down figures and formulæ on anything near at hand.

As there was only one chair in the room, Sarakoff eventually thrust me into it, while he sat down on the great beast—whom he called Belshazzar—and told me over and over again how glad he was to see me. And this warmth of his was pleasant to me.

"Are you experimenting on Belshazzar?" I asked at length.

He nodded, and smiled enigmatically.

"He is two hundred years old," he said. "I want to get at his secret."

That was the first positive proof I got of the line of research Sarakoff was intent upon, although, reading between the lines of his many publications, I had guessed something of it.

In every way, Sarakoff was a complete contrast to me. Tall, lean, black-bearded and deep-voiced, careless of public opinion and prodigal in ideas, he was just my antithesis. He was possessed of immense energy. His tousled black hair, moustaches and beard seemed to bristle with it; it shone in his pale blue eyes. He was full of sudden violence, flinging test-tubes across the laboratory, shouting strange songs, striding about snapping his fingers. There was no repose in him. At first I was a little afraid of him, but the feeling wore off. He spoke English fluently, because when a boy he had been at school in London.

3

I will not enter upon a detailed account of our conversation that first morning in Russia, when the snow lay thick on the roofs of the city, and the ferns of frost sparkled on the window-panes of the laboratory. Briefly, we found ourselves at one over many problems of human research, and I congratulated myself on the fact that in communicating the account of the miracle at St. Dane's Hospital to Sarakoff alone, I had done wisely. He was wonderfully enthusiastic.

"That discovery of yours has furnished the key to the great riddle I had set myself," he exclaimed, striding to and fro. "We will astonish the world, my friend. It is only a question of time."

"But what is the riddle you speak of?" I asked.

"I will tell you soon. Have patience!" he cried. He came towards me impulsively and shook my hand. "We shall find it beyond a doubt, and we will call it the Sarakoff-Harden Bacillus! What do you think of that?"

I was somewhat mystified. He sat down again on the back of the tortoise, smoking in his ferocious manner and smiling and nodding to himself. I though it best to let him disclose his plans in his own way, and kept back the many eager questions that rose to my lips.

"It seems to me," said Sarakoff suddenly, "that England would be the best place to try the experiment. There's a telegraph everywhere, reporters in every village, and enough newspapers to carpet every square inch of the land. In a word, it's a first-class place to watch the results of an experiment."

"On a large scale?"

"On a gigantic scale—an experiment, ultimately, on the world."

I was puzzled and was anxious to draw him into fuller details.

"It would begin in England?" I asked carelessly.

He nodded.

"But it would spread. You remember how the last big outbreak of influenza, which started in this country, spread like wildfire until the waves, passing east and west, met on the other side of the globe? That was a big experiment."

"Of nature," I added.

He did not reply.

"An experiment of nature, you mean?" I urged. At the time of the last big outburst of influenza which began in Russia, Sarakoff must have been a student. Did he know anything about the origin of the mysterious and fatal visitation?

"Yes, of nature," he replied at last, but not in a tone that satisfied me. His manner intrigued me so much that I felt inclined

4

to pursue the subject, but at that moment we were interrupted in a singular way.

The door burst open, and into the room rushed a motley crowd of men. Most of them were young students, but here and there I saw older men, and at the head of the mob was a white-bearded individual, wearing an astrachan cap, who brandished a copy of some Russian periodical in his hand.

Belshazzar drew in his head with a hiss that I could hear even above the clamour of this intrusion.

A furious colloquy began, which I could not understand, since it was in Russian. Sarakoff stood facing the angry crowd coolly enough, but that he was inwardly roused to a dangerous degree, I could tell from his gestures. The copy of the periodical was much in evidence. Fists were shaken freely. The aged, white-bearded leader worked himself up into a frenzy and finally jumped on the periodical, stamping it under his feet until he was out of breath.

Then this excited band trooped out of the room and left us in peace.

"What is it?" I asked when their steps had died away.

Sarakoff shrugged his shoulders and then laughed. He picked up the battered periodical and pointed to an article in it.

"I published a manifesto this morning—that is all," he remarked airily.

"What sort of manifesto?"

"On the origin of death." He sat down on Belshazzar's broad back and twisted his moustaches. "You see, Harden, I believe that in a few more years death will only exist as an uncertain element, appearing rarely, as an unnatural and exceptional incident. Life will be limitless; and the length of years attained by Belshazzar will seem as nothing."

It is curious how the spirit of a new discovery broods over the world like a capricious being, animating one investigator here, another there; partially revealing itself in this continent, disclosing another of its secrets in that, until all the fragments when fitted together make up the whole wonder. It seems that my discovery, coupled with the results of his own unpublished researches, had led Sarakoff to make that odd manifesto. Our combined work, although carried out independently, had given the firm groundwork of an amazing theory which Sarakoff had been maturing in his excited brain for many long years.

Sarakoff translated the manifesto to me. It was a trifle bombastic, and its composition appeared to me vague. No wonder it had roused hostility among his colleagues, I thought, as Sarakoff walked about, declaiming with outstretched arm. Put as briefly as possible, Sarakoff held all disease as due to germs of one sort or another; and decay of bodily tissue he regarded in the same light. In such a theory I stood beside him.

He continued to translate from the soiled and torn periodical, waving his arm majestically.

"We have only to eliminate all germs from the world to banish disease and decay—and death. Such an end can be attained in one way alone; a way which is known only to me, thanks to a magnificent series of profound investigations. I announce, therefore, that the disappearance of death from this planet can be anticipated with the utmost confidence. Let us make preparations. Let us consider our laws. Let us examine our resources. Let us, in short, begin the reconstruction of society."

"Good heavens!" I exclaimed, and sat staring at him.

He twirled his moustaches and observed me with shining eyes.

"What do you think of it?"

I shrugged my shoulders helplessly.

"Surely it is far fetched?"

"Not a bit of it. Now listen to me carefully. I'll give you, step by step, the whole matter." He walked up and down for some minutes and then suddenly stopped beside me and thumped me on the back. "There's not a flaw in it!" he cried. "It's magnificent. My dear fellow, death is only a failure in human perfection. There's nothing mysterious in it. Religion has made a ridiculous fuss about it. There's nothing more mysterious in it than there is in a badly-oiled engine wearing out. Now listen. I'm going to begin...."

I listened, fascinated.

CHAPTER III

THE BUTTERFLIES

Two years passed by after my return to London without special incident, save that my black cat died. My work as a consulting physician occupied most of my time. In the greater world beyond my consulting-room door life went on undisturbed by any thought of the approaching upheaval, full of the old tragedies of ambition and love and sickness. But sometimes as I examined my patients and listened to their tales of suffering and pain, a curious contraction of the heart would come upon me at the thought that perhaps some day, not so very far remote, all the endless cycle of disease and misery would cease, and a new dawn of hope burst with blinding radiance upon weary humanity. And then a mood of unbelief would darken my mind and I would view the creation of the bacillus as an idle and vain dream, an illusion never to be realized....

One evening as I sat alone before my study fire, my servant entered and announced there was a visitor to see me.

"Show him in here," I said, thinking he was probably a late patient who had come on urgent business.

A moment later Professor Sarakoff himself was shown in.

I rose with a cry of welcome and clasped his hand.

"My dear fellow, why didn't you let me know you were coming?" I cried.

He smiled upon me with a mysterious brightness.

"Harden," he said in a low voice, as if afraid of being heard, "I came on a sudden impulse. I wanted to show you something. Wait a moment."

He went out into the hall and returned bearing a square box in his hands. He laid it on the table and then carefully closed the door.

"It is the first big result of my experiments," he whispered. He opened the box and drew out a glass case covered over with white muslin.

He stepped back from the table and looked at me triumphantly.

"What is it?" I asked.

"Lift up the muslin."

I did so. On the wooden floor of the glass case were a great number of dark objects. At first I thought they were some kind of grub, and then on closer inspection I saw what they were.

7

"Butterflies!" I exclaimed.

He held up a warning finger and tiptoed to the door. He opened it suddenly and seemed relieved to find no one outside.

"Hush!" he said, closing the door again. "Yes, they are butterflies." He came back to the table and gave one of the glass panels a tap with his finger. The butterflies stirred and some spread their wings. They were a brilliant greenish purple shot with pale blue. "Yes, they are butterflies."

I peered at them.

"The specimen is unknown in England as far as I know."

"Quite so. They are peculiar to Russia."

"But what are you doing with them?" I asked.

He continued to smile.

"Do you notice anything remarkable about these butterflies?"

"No," I said after prolonged observation, "I can't say I do ... save that they are not denizens of this country."

"I think we might christen them," he said. "Let us call them Lepidoptera Sarakoffii." He tapped the glass again and watched the insects move. "But they are very remarkable," he continued. "Do they appear healthy to you?"

"Perfectly."

"You agree, then, that they are in good condition?"

"They seem to be in excellent condition."

"No signs of decay—or disease?"

"None."

He nodded.

"And yet," he said thoughtfully, "they should be, according to natural law, a mass of decayed tissue."

"Ah!" I looked at him with dawning comprehension. "You mean——?"

"I mean that they should have died long ago."

"How long do they live normally?"

"About twenty to thirty hours. At the outside their life is not more than thirty-six hours. These are somewhat older."

I gazed at the little creatures crawling aimlessly about. Aimless, did I say? There they were, filling up the floor of the glass case, moving with difficulty, getting in each other's way, sprawling and colliding, apparently without aim or purpose. At that spectacle my thoughts might well have taken a leap into the future and seen, instead of a crowded mass of butterflies, a crowded mass of humanity. I asked Sarakoff a question.

"How old are they?" I expected to hear they had existed perhaps a day or two beyond their normal limit.

"They are almost exactly a year old," was the reply. I stared, marvelling. A year old! I bent down, gazing at the turbulent restless mass of gaudy colour. A year old—and still vital and healthy!

"You mean these insects have lived a whole year?" I exclaimed, still unconvinced.

He nodded.

"But that is a miracle!"

"It is, proportionately, equal to a man living twenty-five thousand years instead of the normal seventy."

"You don't suggest——?"

He replaced the muslin covering and took out his pipe and tobacco pouch. Absurd, outrageous ideas crowded to my mind. Was it, then, possible that our dream was to become reality?

"I don't suppose they'll live much longer," I stammered.

He was silent until he had lit his pipe.

"If you met a man who had lived twenty-five thousand years, would you be inclined to tell me he would not live much longer, simply on general considerations?"

I could not find a satisfactory answer.

As a matter of fact the question scarcely conveyed anything to me. One can realize only by reference to familiar standards. The idea of a man who has lived one hundred and fifty years is to me a more realistic curiosity than the idea of a man twenty-five thousand years old. But I caught a glimpse, as it were, of strange figures, moving about in a colourless background, with calm gestures, slow speeches, silences perhaps a year in length. The familiar outline of London crumbled suddenly away, the blotches of shadow and the coloured shafts of light striking between the gaps in the crowds, the violet-lit tubes, the traffic, faded into the conception of twenty-five thousand years. All this many-angled, many-coloured modern spectacle that was a few thousand years removed from cave dwellings, was rolled flat and level, merging into this grey formless carpet of time.

Next morning Sarakoff returned to Russia, bearing with him the wonderful butterflies, and for many months I heard nothing from him. But before he went he told me that he would return soon.

"I have only one step further to take and the ideal germ will be created, Harden. Then we poor mortals will realize the dream that has haunted us since the beginning of time. We will attain immortality, and the fear of death, round which everything is built, will vanish. We will become gods!"

"Or devils, Sarakoff," I murmured.

CHAPTER IV

THE SIX TUBES

One night, just as I entered my house, the telephone bell in the hall rang sharply. I picked up the receiver impatiently, for I was tired with the long day's work.

"Is that Dr. Harden?"

"Yes."

"Can you come down to Charing Cross Station at once? The station-master is speaking."

"An accident?"

"No. We wish you to identify a person who has arrived by the boat-train. The police are detaining him as a suspect. He gave your name as a reference. He is a Russian."

"All right. I'll come at once."

I hung up the receiver and told the servant to whistle for a taxi-cab. Ten minutes later I was picking my way through the crowds on the platform to the station-master's office. I entered, and found a strange scene being enacted. On one side of a table stood Sarakoff, very flushed, with shining eyes, clasping a black bag tightly to his breast. On the other side stood a group of four men, the station-master, a police officer, a plain clothes man and an elderly gentleman in white spats. The last was pointing an accusing finger at Sarakoff.

"Open that bag and we'll believe you!" he shouted.

Sarakoff glared at him defiantly.

I recognized his accuser at once. It was Lord Alberan, the famous Tory obstructionist.

"Anarchist!" Lord Alberan's voice rang out sharply. He took out a handkerchief and mopped his face.

"Arrest him!" he said to the constable with an air of satisfaction. "I knew he was an anarchist the moment I set eyes on him at Dover. There is an infernal machine in that bag. The man reeks of vodka. He is mad."

"Idiot," exclaimed Sarakoff, with great vehemence. "I drink nothing but water."

"He wishes to destroy London," said Lord Alberan coldly. "There is enough dynamite in that bag to blow the whole of Trafalgar Square into fragments. Arrest him instantly."

I stepped forward from the shadows by the door. Sarakoff uttered a cry of pleasure.

"Ah, Harden, I knew you would come. Get me out of this stupid situation!"

"What is the matter?" I asked, glancing at the station-master. He explained briefly that Lord Alberan and Sarakoff had travelled up in the same compartment from Dover, and that Sarakoff's strange restlessness and excited movements had roused Lord Alberan's suspicions. As a consequence Sarakoff had been detained for examination.

"If he would open his bag we should be satisfied," added the station-master. I looked at my friend significantly.

"Why not open it?" I asked. "It would be simplest."

My words had the effect of quieting the excited professor. He put the bag on the table, and placed his hands on the top of it.

"Very well," he said slowly, "I will open it, since my friend Dr. Harden has requested me to do so."

"Stand back!" cried Lord Alberan, flinging out his arms. "We may be so much dust flying over London in a moment."

Sarakoff took out a key and unlocked the bag. There was silence for a moment, only broken by hurrying footsteps on the platform without. Then Lord Alberan stepped cautiously forward.

He saw the worn canvas lining of the bag. He took a step nearer and saw a wooden rack, fitted in the interior, containing six glass tubes whose mouths were stopped with plugs of cotton wool.

"You see, there is nothing important there," said Sarakoff with a smile. "These objects are of purely scientific interest." He took out one of the tubes and held it up to the light. It was half full of a semi-transparent jelly-like mass, faintly blue in colour. The detective, the policeman and the station official clustered round, their faces turned up to the light and their eyes fixed on the tube. The Russian looked at them narrowly, and reading nothing but dull wonderment in their expressions, began to speak again.

"Yes—the Bacillus Pyocyaneus," he said, with a faint mocking smile and a side glance at me. "It is occasionally met with in man and is easily detected by the blue bye-product it gives off while growing." He twisted the tube slowly round. "It is quite an interesting culture," he continued idly. "Do you observe the uniform distribution of the growth and the absence of any sign of liquefaction in the medium?"

Lord Alberan cleared his throat.

"I—er—I think we owe you an apology," he said. "My suspicions were unfounded. However, I did my duty to my country by having you examined. You must admit your conduct was suspicious—highly suspicious, sir!"

Sarakoff replaced the tube and locked the bag. Lord Alberan marched to the door and held it open.

"We need not detain you, sir," said the detective. The policeman squared his shoulders and hitched up his belt. The station official looked nervous.

Dr. Sarakoff, with a gesture of indifference, picked up the bag and, taking me by the arm, passed out on to the brilliantly-lit platform. "Pyocyaneus," he muttered in my ear; "pyocyaneus, indeed! Confound the fellow. He might have got me into no end of trouble if he had known the truth, Harden."

"But what is it?" I asked. "What have you got in the bag?"

He stopped under a sizzling arc-lamp outside the station.

"The bag," he said touching the worn leather lovingly, "contains six tubes of the Sarakoff-Harden bacillus. Yes, I have added your name to it. I will make your name immortal—by coupling it with mine."

"But what is the Sarakoff-Harden bacillus?" I cried.

He struck an attitude under the viperish glare of the lamp and smiled. He certainly did look like an anarchist at the moment. He loomed over me, huge, satanic, inscrutable.

A thrill, almost of fear, passed over me. I glanced round in some apprehension. Under an archway near by I saw Lord Alberan looking fixedly at us. The expression of suspicion had returned to his face.

"You mean——?" He nodded. I gulped a little. "You really have——?" He continued to nod. "Then we can try the great experiment?" I whispered, dry throated.

"At once!" The detective passed us, brushing against my shoulder. I caught Sarakoff by the arm.

"Look here—we must get away," I muttered. I felt like a criminal. Sarakoff clasped the bag firmly under his free arm. We began to walk hurriedly away. Our manner was furtive. Once I looked back and saw Alberan talking, with excited gestures, to the detective. They were both looking in our direction. The impulse to run possessed me. "Quick," I exclaimed, "there's a taxi. Jump in. Drive to Harley Street—like the devil."

Inside the cab I lay back, my mind in a whirl.

"We begin the experiment to-morrow," said Sarakoff at last. "Have you made plans as I told you?"

"Yes—yes. Of course. Only I never believed it possible." I controlled myself and sat up. "I fixed on Birmingham. It seemed best—but I never dreamed——"

12

"Good!" he exclaimed. "Birmingham, then!"

"Their water supply comes from Wales."

We spoke no more till I turned the key of my study door behind me. It was in this way that the germ, which made so vast and strange an impression on the course of the world's history, first reached England. It had lain under the very nose of Lord Alberan, who opposed everything new automatically. Yet it, the newest of all things, escaped his vigilance.

We decided to put our plans into action without delay, and next morning we set off, carrying with us the precious tubes of the Sarakoff-Harden bacillus. Throughout the long journey we scarcely spoke to each other. Each of us was absorbed in his picture of the future effects of the germ.

There was one strange fact that Sarakoff had told me the night before, and that I had verified. The bacillus was ultra-microscopical—that is, it could not be seen, even with the highest power, under the microscope. Its presence was only to be detected by the blue stain it gave off during its growth.

CHAPTER V

THE GREAT AQUEDUCT

The Birmingham reservoirs are a chain of lakes artificially produced by damming up the River Elan, a tributary of the Wye. The great aqueduct which carries the water from the Elan, eighty miles across country, travelling through hills and bridging valleys, runs past Ludlow and Cleobury Mortimer, through the Wyre Forest to Kidderminster, and on to Birmingham itself through Frankley, where there is a large storage reservoir from which the water is distributed.

The scenery was bleak and desolate. Before us the sun was sinking in a flood of crimson light. We walked briskly, the long legs of the Russian carrying him swiftly over the uneven ground while I trotted beside him. Before the last rays of the sun had died away we saw the black outline of the Caban Loch dam before us, and caught the sheen of water beyond. On the north lay the river Elan and on the south the steep side of a mountain towered up against the luminous sky. The road runs along the left bank of the river bounded by a series of bold and abrupt crags that rise to a height of some eight hundred feet above the level of the water. Just below the Caban Dam is a house occupied by an inspector in charge of the gauge apparatus that is used to measure the outflow of water from the huge natural reservoirs. The lights from his house twinkled through the growing darkness as we drew near, and we skirted it by a short detour and pressed on.

"How long does water take to get from here to Birmingham?" asked Sarakoff as we climbed up to the edge of the first lake.

"It travels about a couple of miles an hour," I replied. "So that means about a day and a half."

We spoke in low voices, for we were afraid of detection. The presence of two visitors at that hour might well have attracted attention.

"A day and a half! Then the bacillus has a long journey to take." He stopped at the margin of the water and stared across the shadowy lake. "Yes, it has a long journey to take, for it will go round the whole world."

The last glow in the sky tinted the calm sheet of water a deep blood colour. Sarakoff opened his bag and took out a couple of tubes.

14

He pulled the cotton-wool plugs out of the tubes, and with a long wire, loosened the gelatinous contents. Then, inverting the tubes he flung them into the lake close to the beginning of the huge aqueduct.

I stared as the tubes vanished from sight, feeling that it was too late to regret what had now been done, for nothing could collect those millions of bacilli, that had been set free in the water. Already some of them had perhaps entered the dark cavernous mouth of the first culvert to start on their slow journey to Birmingham. The light faded from the sky and darkness spread swiftly over the lake. Sarakoff emptied the remaining tubes calmly and then turned his footsteps in the direction of Rhayader. I waited a moment longer in the deep silence of that lonely spot; and then with a shiver followed my friend. The bacillus had been let loose on the world.

CHAPTER VI

THE ATTITUDE OF MR. THORNDUCK

We reached London next day in the afternoon. I felt exhausted and could scarcely answer Sarakoff, who had talked continuously during the journey.

But his theory had interested me. The Russian had revealed much of his character, under the stress of excitement. He spoke of the coming of Immortality in the light of a physical boon to mankind. He seemed to see in his mind's eye a great picture of comfort and physical enjoyment and of a humanity released from the grim spectres of disease and death, and ceaselessly pursuing pleasure.

"I love life," he remarked. "I love fame and success. I love comfort, ease, laughter, and companionship. The whole of Nature is beautiful to me, and a beautiful woman is Nature's best reward. Now that the dawn of Immortality is at hand, Harden, we must set about reorganizing the world so that it may yield the maximum of pleasure."

"But surely there will be some limit to pleasure?" I objected.

"Why? Can't you see that is just what there will not be?" he cried excitedly. "We are going to do away with the confining limits. Your imagination is too cramped! You sit there, huddled up in a corner, as if we had let loose a dreadful plague on Birmingham!"

"It may prove to be so," I muttered. I do not think I had any clear idea as to the future, but there is a natural machinery in the mind that doubts golden ages and universal panaceas. Call it superstition if you will, but man's instinct tells him he cannot have uninterrupted pleasure without paying for it. I said as much to the Russian.

He gave vent to a roar of laughter.

"You have all the caution and timidity of your race," he said. "You are fearful even in your hour of deliverance. My friend, it is impossible to conceive, even faintly, of the change that will come over us towards the meaning of life. Can't you see that, as soon as the idea of Immortality gets hold of people, they will devote all their energies to making their earth a paradise? Why, it is obvious. They will then know that there is no other paradise."

He took out his watch and made a calculation. His face became flushed.

"The bacillus has travelled forty-two miles towards Birmingham," he said, just as our train drew in to the London terminus.

I was busy with patients until dinner-time and did not see anything of Sarakoff. While working, my exhaustion and anxiety wore off, and were replaced by a mild exhilaration. One of my patients was a professor of engineering at a northern university; a brilliant young man, who, but for physical disease, had the promise of a great career before him. He had been sent to me, after having made a round of the consultants, to see if I could give him any hope as to the future. I went into his case carefully, and then addressed him a question.

"What is your own view of your case, Mr. Thornduck?"

He looked surprised. His face relaxed, and he smiled. I suppose he detected a message of hope in my expression.

"I have been told by half-a-dozen doctors that I have not long to live, Dr. Harden," he replied. "But it is very difficult for me to grasp that view. I find that I behave as if nothing were the matter. I still go on working. I still see goals far ahead. Death is just a word—frequently uttered, it is true—but meaningless. What am I to do?"

"Go on working."

"And am I to expect only a short lease of life?"

I rose from my writing-table and walked to the hearth. A surge of power came over me as I thought of the bacillus which was so silently and steadily advancing on Birmingham.

"Do you believe in miracles?" I asked.

"That is an odd question." He reflected for a time. "No, I don't think so. All one is taught now-a-days is in a contrary direction, isn't it?"

"Yes, but our knowledge only covers a very small field—perhaps an artificially isolated one, too."

"Then you think only a miracle will save my life?"

I nodded and gazed at him.

"You seem amused," he remarked quietly.

"I am not amused, Mr. Thornduck. I am very happy."

"Does my case interest you?"

"Extremely. As a case, you are typical. Your malady is invariably fatal. It is only one of the many maladies that we know to be fatal, while we remain ignorant of all else. Under ordinary circumstances, you would have before you about three years of reasonable health and sanity."

"And then?"

"Well, after that you would be somewhat helpless. You would

17

begin to employ that large section of modern civilization that deals with the somewhat helpless."

I began to warm to my theme, and clasped my hands behind my back.

"Yes, you would pass into that class that disproves all theories of a kindly Deity, and you would become an undergraduate in the vast and lamentable University of Suffering, through whose limitless corridors we medical men walk with weary footsteps. Ah, if only an intelligent group of scientists had had the construction of the human body to plan! Think what poor stuff it is! Think how easy it would have been to make it more enduring! The cell—what a useless fragile delicacy! And we are made of millions of these useless fragile delicacies."

To my surprise he laughed with great amusement. He stood there, young, pleasant, and smiling. I stared at him with a curious uneasiness. For the moment I had forgotten what it had been my intention to say. The dawn of Immortality passed out of my mind, and I found myself gazing, as it were, on something strangely mysterious.

"Your religion helps you?" I hazarded.

"Religion?" He mused for a moment. "Don't you think there is some meaning behind our particular inevitable destinies—that we may perhaps have earned them?"

"Nonsense! It is all the cruel caprice of Nature, and nothing else."

"Oh, come, Dr. Harden, you surely take a larger view. Do you think the short existence we have here is all the chance of activity we ever have? That I have a glimpse of engineering, and you have a short phase of doctoring on this planet, and that then we have finished all experience?"

"Certainly. It would not be possible to take any other view— horrible."

"But you believe in some theory of evolution—of slow upward progress?"

"Yes, of course. That is proved beyond all doubt."

"And yet you think it applies only to the body—to the instrument—and not to the immaterial side of us?"

I stared at him in astonishment.

"I do not think there is any immaterial side, Mr. Thornduck."

He smiled.

"A very unsatisfying view, surely?" he remarked.

"Unsatisfying, perhaps, but sound science," I retorted.

"Sound?" He pondered for an instant. "Can a thing be sound

and unsatisfying at the same time? When I see a machine that's ugly—that's unsatisfying from the artist's point of view—I always know it's wrongly planned and inefficient. Don't you think it's the same with theories of life?" He took out his watch and glanced at it. "But I must not keep you. Good-bye, Dr. Harden."

He went to the door, nodded, and left the room before I recalled that I meant to hint to him that a miracle was going to happen, and save his life. I remained on the hearth-rug, wondering what on earth he meant.

CHAPTER VII

LEONORA

I found a note in the hall from Sarakoff asking me to come round to the Pyramid Restaurant at eight o'clock to meet a friend of his. It was a crisp clear evening, and I decided to walk. There were two problems on my mind. One was the outlook of Sarakoff, which even I deemed to be too materialistic. The other was the attitude of young Thornduck, which was obviously absurd.

In my top hat and solemn frock-coat I paced slowly down Harley Street.

Thornduck talked as if suffering, as if all that side of existence which the Blue Germ was to do away with, were necessary and salutary. Sarakoff spoke as if pleasure was the only aim of life. Now, though sheer physical pleasure had never entered very deeply into my life, I had never denied the fact that it was the only motive of the majority of my patients. For what was all our research for? Simply to mitigate suffering; and that is another way of saying that it was to increase physical well-being. Why, then, did Sarakoff's views appear extreme to me? What was there in my composition that whispered a doubt when I had the doctrine of maximum pleasure painted with glowing enthusiasm by the Russian in the train that afternoon?

I moved into Oxford Street deeply pondering. The streets were crowded, and from shop windows there streamed great wedges of white and yellow light. The roar of traffic was round me. The 'buses were packed with men and women returning late from business, or on the way to seek relaxation in the city's amusements. I passed through the throng as through a coloured mist of phantoms. My eyes fastened on the faces of those who passed by. Who could really doubt the doctrine of pleasure? Which one of those people would hesitate to plunge into the full tide of the senses, did not the limitations of the body prevent him?

I crossed Piccadilly Circus with a brisker step. It was no use worrying over questions which could not be examined scientifically. The only really important question in life was to be a success.

The brilliant entrance of the Pyramid Restaurant was before me, and within, standing on the marble floor, I saw the tall figure of the Russian.

Sarakoff greeted me with enthusiasm. He was wearing

evening-dress with a white waistcoat, and the fact perturbed me. I put my hat and stick in the cloakroom.

"Who is coming?" I asked anxiously.

"Leonora," he whispered. "I only found out she was in London this afternoon. I met her when I was strolling in the Park while you were busy with your patients."

"But who is Leonora?" I asked. "And can I meet her in this state?"

"Oh, never mind about your dress. You are a busy doctor and she will understand. Leonora is the most marvellous woman in the world. I intend to make her marry me."

"Is she English?" I stammered.

He laughed.

"Little man, you look terrified, as usual. You are always terrified. It is your habit. No, Leonora is not English. She is European. If you went out into the world of amusement a little more—and it would be good for you—you would know that she has the most exquisite voice in the history of civilization. She transcends the nightingale because her body is beautiful. She transcends the peacock because her voice is beautiful. She is, in fact, worthy of every homage, and you will meet her in a short time. Like all perfect things she is late."

He took out his watch and glanced at the door.

"You are an extraordinary person, Sarakoff," I observed, after watching him a moment. "Will you answer me a rather intimate question?"

"Certainly."

"What precisely do you mean when you say you intend to make the charming lady marry you?"

"Precisely what I say. She loves fame. So far I have been unsuccessful, because she does not think I am famous enough."

"How do you intend to remedy that?"

He stared at me in amazement.

"Do you think that any people have ever been so famous as you and I will be in a few days?"

I looked away and studied the bright throng of visitors in the hall.

"In a few days?" I asked. "Are you not a trifle optimistic? Don't you think that it will take months before the possibilities and meaning of the germ are properly realized?"

"Rubbish," exclaimed Sarakoff. "You are a confirmed pessimist. You are impossible, Harden. You are a mass of doubts

21

and apprehensions. Ah, here is Leonora at last. Is she not marvellous?"

I looked towards the entrance. I saw a woman of medium height, very fair, dressed in some soft clinging material of a pale primrose colour. From a shoulder hung a red satin cloak. Round her neck was a string of large pearls, and in her hair was a jewelled osprey. She presented a striking appearance and I gained the impression of some northern spirit in her that shone out of her eyes with the brilliancy of ice.

Sarakoff strode forward, and the contrast that these two afforded was extraordinary. Tall, dark, warm and animated, he stood beside her, and stooped to kiss her hand. She gazed at him with a smile so slight that it seemed scarcely to disturb the perfect symmetry of her face. He began to talk, moving his whole body constantly and making gestures with his arms, with a play of different expressions in his face. She listened without moving, save that her eyes wandered slowly round the large hall. At length Sarakoff beckoned to me.

I approached somewhat awkwardly and was introduced.

"Leonora," said the Russian, "this is a little English doctor with a very large brain. He was closely connected with the great discovery of which I am going to tell you something to-night at dinner. He is my friend and his name is Richard Harden."

"I like your name," said Leonora, in a clear soft voice.

I took her hand. We passed into the restaurant. It was one of those vast pleasure-palaces of music, scent, colour and food that abounded in London. An orchestra was playing somewhere high aloft. The luxury of these establishments was always sounding a curious warning deep down in my mind. But then, as Sarakoff had said, I am a pessimist, and if I were to say that I have noticed that nature often becomes very prodigal and lavish just before she takes away and destroys, I would be uttering, perhaps, one of the many half-truths in which the pessimistic spirit delights.

Our table was in a corner at an agreeable distance from the orchestra. Sarakoff placed Leonora between him and myself. Attentive waiters hurried to serve us; and the eyes of everyone in our immediate neighbourhood were turned in our direction. Leonora did not appear to be affected by the interest she aroused. She flung her cloak on the back of her chair, put her elbows on the table, and gazed at the Russian intently.

"Tell me of your discovery, Alexis."

He smiled, enchanted.

"I shall be best able to give you some idea of what our

22

discovery means if I begin by telling you that I am going to read your character. Does that interest you?"

She nodded. Then she turned to me and studied me for a moment.

"No, Alexis. Let Richard read my character first."

I blushed successfully.

"Why do you blush?" she asked with some interest.

"He blushed because of your unpardonable familiarity in calling him Richard," laughed Sarakoff.

"I shall be most happy, Leonora," I stammered, making an immense effort, and longing for the waiter to bring the champagne. "But I am not good at the art."

"But you must try."

I saw no way out of the predicament. Sarakoff's eyes were twinkling roguishly, so I began, keeping my gaze on the table.

"You have a well-controlled character, with a considerable power of knowing exactly what you want to do with your life, and you come from the North. I fancy you sleep badly."

"How do you know I sleep badly?" she challenged.

"Your eyes are a clear frosty blue, and you are of rather slight build. I am merely speaking from my own experience as a doctor."

I suppose my words were not particularly gracious or well-spoken. Leonora simply nodded and leaned back from the table.

"Now, Alexis, tell me about myself," she said.

My glass now contained champagne and I decided to allow that wizard to take charge of my affairs for a time.

"Leonora, you are one of those women who visit this dull planet from time to time for reasons best known to themselves. I think you must come from Venus, or one of the asteroids; or it may be from Sirius. From the beginning you knew you were not like ordinary people."

"Alexis," she drawled, "you are boring me."

"Capital!" said Sarakoff. "Now we will descend to facts, as our friend here did. You are the most inordinately vain, ambitious, cold-hearted woman in Europe, Leonora. You value yourself before everything. You think your voice and your beauty cannot be beaten, and you are right. Now if I were to tell you that your voice and your beauty could be preserved, year after year, without any change, what would you think?"

A kind of fierce vitality sprang into her face.

"What do you mean?" she asked quietly. "Have you discovered the elixir of youth?"

He nodded. She laid her hand on his arm.

"How long does its effect last?"

"Well—for a considerable time."

"You are certain?"

"Absolutely."

She leaned towards him.

"You will let no one else have it, Alexis," she asked softly. "Only me?"

Sarakoff glanced at me.

"Leonora, you are very selfish."

"Of course."

"Well, you are not the only person who is going to have the elixir. The whole world is going to have it."

I watched her with absorbed attention. She seemed to accept the idea of an elixir of youth without any incredulity, and did not find anything extraordinary in the fact of its discovery. In that respect, I fancied, she was typical of a large class of women—that class that thinks a doctor is a magician, or should be. But when Sarakoff said that the whole world was going to have the elixir, a spasm of anger shewed for a moment in her face. She lowered her eyes.

"This is unkind of you, Alexis. Why should not just you and I have the elixir?" She raised her eyes and turned them directly on Sarakoff. "Why not?" she murmured.

The Russian flushed slightly.

"Leonora, it must either not be, or else the whole world must have it. It can't be confined. It must spread. It's a germ. We have let it loose in Birmingham."

She shuddered.

"A germ? What does he mean?" She turned to me.

"It's a germ that will do away with all disease and decay," I said.

"It will make me younger?"

"Of that I am uncertain. It will more probably fix us where we are."

The Russian nodded in confirmation of my view. Leonora considered for a while. I could see nothing in her appearance that she could have wished altered, but she seemed dissatisfied.

"I should have preferred it to make us all a little younger," she said decidedly. Her total lack of the sense of miracles astonished me. She behaved as if Sarakoff had told her that we had discovered a new kind of soap or a new patent food. "But I am glad you have found it, Alexis," she continued. "It will certainly make you famous. That will be nice, but I am sorry you should have given the elixir to

Birmingham first. Birmingham is in no need of an elixir, my friend. You should have put something else in their water-supply." She turned to me and examined me with calm criticism. "What a pity you didn't discover the elixir when you were younger, Richard. Your hair is grey at the temples." A clear laugh suddenly came from her. "What a lot of jealously there will be, Alexis. The old ones will be so envious of the young. Think how Madame Réaour will rage—and Betty, and the Signora—all my friends—oh, I feel quite glad now that it doesn't make people younger. You are sure it won't?"

"I don't think so," said Sarakoff, watching her through half-closed lids. "No, I think you are safe, Leonora."

"And my voice?"

"It will preserve that ... indefinitely, I think."

She was arrested by the new idea. She looked into the distance and fingered the pearls at her throat.

"Then I shall become the most famous singer in the whole world," she murmured. "And I shall have all the money I want. My friend, you have done me a service. I will not forget it." She looked at him and laughed slightly. "But I do not think you have done the world a service. A great many people will not like the germ. No, they will desire to get rid of it, Alexis."

She shuddered a little. I stared at her.

"I think you are mistaken," said Alexis, gruffly.

She shook her head.

"Come, let us finish dinner quickly and I will take you both to my flat and sing to you a little."

Leonora's flat was in Whitehall Court, and of its luxury I need not speak. I must confess to the fact that, sober and timid as is my nature, I thoroughly enjoyed the atmosphere. Leonora was generous. Her voice was exquisite. I sat on a deep couch of green satin and gazed at a Chinese idol cut in green jade, that stood on a neighbouring table, with all my senses lulled by the charm of her singing. The sense of responsibility fell away from me like severed cords. I became pagan as I lolled there, a creature of sensuous feeling. Sarakoff lay back in a deep chair in the shadow with his eyes fixed on Leonora. We were both in a kind of delicious drowsiness when the opening of the door roused us.

Leonora stopped abruptly. With some difficulty I removed my gaze from the Chinese figure, which had hypnotized me, and looked round resentfully.

Lord Alberan was standing in the doorway. He seemed surprised to find that Leonora had visitors. I could not help marking a slight air of proprietorship in his manner.

"I am afraid I am interrupting," he said smoothly. He crossed to the piano and leant over Leonora. "You got my telegram?"

"No," she replied; "I did not even know you had returned from France."

"I came the day before yesterday. I had to go down to Maltby Towers. I came up to town to-day and wired you on the way."

He straightened himself and turned towards us. Leonora rose and came down the room. We rose.

"Geoffrey," she said, drawling slightly, "I want to introduce you to two friends of mine. They will soon be very famous—more famous than you are—because they have discovered a germ that is going to keep us all young."

Lord Alberan glanced at me and then looked hard at the Russian. A swiftly passing surprise shewed that he recognized Sarakoff. Leonora mentioned our names casually, took up a cigarette and dropped into a chair.

"Yes," she continued, "these gentlemen have put the germ into the water that supplies Birmingham." She struck a match and lit the cigarette. I noticed she actually smoked very little, but seemed to like to watch the burning cigarette. "Do sit down. What are you standing for, Geoffrey?"

Lord Alberan's attitude relaxed. He had evidently decided on his course of action.

"That is very interesting," he observed, as if he had never seen Sarakoff before. "A germ that is going to keep us all young. It reminds me of the Arabian Nights. I should like to see it."

"You've seen it already," replied Sarakoff, imperturbably.

Lord Alberan's cold eyes looked steadily before him. His mouth tightened.

"Really?"

"You saw it at Charing Cross Station the night before last."

"At Charing Cross Station?"

I tried to signal to the Russian, but he seemed determined to proceed.

"Yes—you thought I was an anarchist. You saw the contents of my bag. Six tubes containing a blue-coloured gelatine. Perhaps, Lord Alberan, you remember now."

"I remember perfectly," he exclaimed, smiling slightly. "Yes, I regret my mistake. One has to be careful."

"Did you think my Alexis was an anarchist?" cried Leonora. "You are the stupidest of Englishmen."

It was obvious that Alberan did not like this. He glanced at a thin gold watch that he carried in his waistcoat pocket.

26

"I will not interrupt you any longer," he remarked gravely. "You are quite occupied, I see, and I much apologize for intruding."

"Don't be still more stupid," she said lazily. "Sit down. Tell me how you like the idea of never dying."

"I am afraid I cannot entertain the idea seriously." He hesitated and then looked firmly at Sarakoff. "Do I understand, sir, that you have actually put some germ into the Birmingham water-supply?"

The Russian nodded.

"You'll hear about it in a day or two," he said quietly.

"You had permission to do this?"

"No, I had no permission."

"Are you aware that you are making a very extraordinary statement, sir?"

"Perfectly."

Lord Alberan became very red. The lower part of his face seemed to expand. His eyes protruded.

"Don't gobble," said Leonora.

"Gobble?" stuttered Alberan, turning upon her. "How dare you say I gobble?"

"But you are gobbling."

"I refuse to stay here another moment. I will leave immediately. As for you, sir, you shall hear from me in course of time. To-morrow I am compelled to go abroad again, but when I return I shall institute a vigorous and detailed enquiry into your movements, which are highly suspicious, sir,—highly suspicious." He moved to the door and then turned. "Mademoiselle, I wish you good-night." He bowed stiffly and went out.

"Thank heaven, I've got rid of him for good," murmured Leonora. "He proposed to me last week, Alexis."

"And what did you say?" asked Sarakoff.

"I said I would see, but things are different now." She turned her eyes straight in his direction. "That is, if you have told me the truth, Alexis. Oh, isn't it wonderful!" She jumped up and threw out her arms. "Suppose that it all comes true, Alexis! Immortality— always to be young and beautiful!"

"It will come true," he said.

She lowered her arms slowly and looked at him.

"I wonder how long love will last?"

CHAPTER VIII

THE BLUE DISEASE

Next day the first news of the Sarakoff-Harden bacillus appeared in a small paragraph in an evening paper, and immediately I saw it, I hurried back to the house in Harley Street where Sarakoff was writing a record of our researches.

"Listen to this," I cried, bursting excitedly into the room. I laid the paper on the table and pointed to the column. "Curious disease among trout in Wales," I read. "In the Elan reservoirs which have long been famed for their magnificent trout, which have recently increased so enormously in size and number that artificial stocking is entirely unnecessary, a curious disease has made its appearance. Fish caught there this morning are reported to have an unnatural bluish tint, and their flesh, when cooked, retains this hue. It is thought that some disease has broken out. Against this theory is the fact that no dead fish have been observed. The Water Committee of the City Council of Birmingham are investigating this matter."

Sarakoff pushed his chair back and twisted it round towards me. For some moments we stared at each other with almost scared expressions. Then a smile passed over the Russian's face.

"Ah, we had forgotten that. A bluish tint! Of course, it was to be expected."

"Yes," I cried, "and what is more, the bluish tint will show itself in every man, woman or child infected with the bacillus. Good heavens, fancy not thinking of that ourselves!"

Sarakoff picked up the paper and read the paragraph for himself. Then he laid it down. "It is strange that one so persistently neglects the obvious in one's calculations. Of course there will be a bluish tint." He leaned back and pulled at his beard. "I should think it will show itself in the whites of the eyes first, just as jaundice shews itself there. Leonora won't like that—it won't suit her colouring. You see that these fish, when cooked, retained the bluish hue. That is very interesting."

"It's very bad luck on the trout."

"Why?"

"After getting the bacillus into their system, they blunder on to a hook and meet their death straight away."

"The bacillus is not proof against death by violence," replied

28

Sarakoff gravely. "That is a factor that will always remain constant. We are agreed in looking on all disease as eventually due to poisons derived from germ activity, but a bang on the head or asphyxiation or prussic acid or a bullet in the heart are not due to a germ. Yes, these poor trout little knew what a future they forfeited when they took the bait."

"The bacillus is in Birmingham by now," I said suddenly. I passed my hand across my brow nervously, and glanced at the manuscript lying before Sarakoff. "You had better keep those papers locked up. I spent an awful day at the hospital. It dawned on me that the whole medical profession will want to tear us in pieces before the year is out."

"In theory they ought not to."

"Who cares for theory, when it is a question of earning a living? As I walked along the street to-day, I could have shrieked aloud when I saw everybody hurrying about as if nothing were going to happen. This is unnerving me. It is so tremendous."

Sarakoff picked up his pen, and traced out a pattern in the blotting-pad before him.

"The Water Committee of Birmingham are investigating the matter," he observed. "It will be amusing to hear their report. What will they think when they make a bacteriological examination of the water in the reservoir? It will stagger them."

The next morning I was down to breakfast before my friend and stood before the fire eagerly scanning the papers. At first I could find nothing that seemed to indicate any further effects of the bacillus. I was in the act of buttering a piece of toast when my eye fell on one of the newspapers lying beside me. A heading in small type caught my eye.

"The measles epidemic in Ludlow." I picked the paper up.

"The severe epidemic of measles which began last week and seemed likely to spread through the entire town, has mysteriously abated. Not only are no further cases reported, but several doctors report that those already attacked have recovered in an incredibly short space of time. Doubt has been expressed by the municipal authorities as to whether the epidemic was really measles."

I adjusted my glasses to read the paragraph again. Then I got up and went into my study. After rummaging in a drawer I pulled out and unrolled a map of England. The course of the aqueduct from Elan to Birmingham was marked by a thin red line. I followed it slowly with the point of my finger and came on the town of Ludlow about half-way along. I stared at it.

"Of course," I whispered at length, my finger still resting on the position of the town. "All these towns on the way are supplied by the aqueduct. I hadn't thought of that. The bacillus is in Ludlow."

For about a minute I did not move. Then I rolled up the map and went up to Sarakoff's bedroom. I met the Russian on the landing on his way to the bathroom.

"The bacillus is in Ludlow," I said in a curiously small voice. I stood on the top stair, holding on to the bannister, my big glasses aslant on my nose, and the map hanging down in my limp grasp.

I had to repeat the sentence before Sarakoff heard me.

"Where's Ludlow?"

I sank on my knees and unrolled the map on the floor and pointed directly with my finger.

Sarakoff went down on all fours and looked at the spot keenly.

"Ah, on the line of the aqueduct! But how do you know it is there?"

"It has cut short an epidemic of measles. The doctors are puzzled."

Sarakoff nodded. He was looking at the names of the other towns that lay on the course of the aqueduct.

"Cleobury-Mortimer," he spelt out. "No news from there?"

"None."

"And none from Birmingham yet?"

"None."

"We'll have news to-morrow." He raised himself on his knees. "Trout and then measles!" he said, and laughed. "This is only the beginning. No wonder the Ludlow doctors are puzzled."

The same evening there was further news of the progress of the bacillus. From Cleobury-Mortimer, ten miles from Ludlow, and twenty from Birmingham, it was reported that the measles epidemic there had been cut short in the same mysterious manner as noticed in Ludlow. But next morning a paragraph of considerable length appeared which I read out in a trembling voice to Sarakoff.

"It was reported a short time ago that the trout in the Elan reservoirs appeared to be suffering from a singular disease, the effect of which was to tint their scales and flesh a delicate bluish colour. The matter is being investigated. In the meanwhile it has been noticed, both in Ludlow and Cleobury-Mortimer, and also in Knighton, that the peculiar bluish tint has appeared amongst the inhabitants. Our correspondent states that it is most marked in the conjunctivæ, or whites of the eyes. There must undoubtedly be some connection between this phenomenon and the condition of the trout in the Elan reservoirs, as all the above-mentioned towns lie close to, and receive water from, the great aqueduct. The most remarkable

30

thing, however, is that the bluish discolouration does not seem to be accompanied by any symptoms of illness in those whom it has affected. No sickness or fever has been observed. It is perhaps nothing more than a curious coincidence that the abrupt cessation of the measles epidemic in Ludlow and Cleobury-Mortimer, reported in yesterday's issue, should have occurred simultaneously with the appearance of bluish discolouration among the inhabitants."

On the same evening, I was returning from the hospital and saw the following words on a poster:—

"Blue Disease in Birmingham."

I bought a paper and scanned the columns rapidly. In the stop-press news I read:—

"The Blue Disease has appeared in Birmingham. Cases are reported all over the city. The Public Health Department are considering what measures should be adopted. The disease seems to be unaccompanied by any dangerous symptoms."

I stood stock-still in the middle of the pavement. A steady stream of people hurrying from business thronged past me. A newspaper boy was shouting something down the street, and as he drew nearer, I heard his hoarse voice bawling out:—

"Blue Disease in Birmingham."

He passed close to me, still bawling, and his voice died away in the distance. Men jostled me and glanced at me angrily.... But I was lost in a dream. The paper dropped from my fingers. In my mind's eye I saw the Sarakoff-Harden bacillus in Birmingham, teeming in every water-pipe in countless billions, swarming in the carafes on dining-room tables, and in every ewer and finger-basin, infecting everything it came in contact with. And the vision of Birmingham and the whole stretch of country up to the Elan watershed passed before me, stained with a vivid blue.

CHAPTER IX

THE MAN FROM BIRMINGHAM

The following day while walking to the hospital, I noticed a group of people down a side street, apparently looking intently at something unusual. I turned aside to see what it was. About twenty persons, mostly errand boys, were standing round a sandwich-board man. At the outskirts of the circle, I raised myself on tip-toe and peered over the heads of those in front. The sandwich-board man's back was towards me.

"What's the matter?" I asked of my neighbour.

"One of the blue freaks from Birmingham," was the reply.

My first impulse was to fly. Here I was in close proximity to my handiwork. I turned and made off a few paces. But curiosity overmastered me, and I came back. The man was now facing me, and I could see him distinctly through a gap in the crowd. It was a thin, unshaven face with straightened features and gaunt cheeks. The eyes were deeply sunken and at that moment turned downwards. His complexion was pale, but I could see a faint bluish tinge suffusing the skin, that gave it a strange, dead look. And then the man lifted his eyes and gazed straight at me. I caught my breath, for under the black eye brows, the whites of the eyes were stained a pure sparrow-egg blue.

"I came from Birmingham yesterday," I heard him saying. "There ain't nothing the matter with me."

"You ought to go to a fever hospital," said someone.

"We don't want that blue stuff in London," added another.

"Perhaps it's catching," said the first speaker.

In a flash everyone had drawn back. The sandwich-board man stood in the centre of the road alone looking sharply round him. Suddenly a wave of rage seemed to possess him. He shook his fist in the air, and even as he shook it, his eyes caught the blue sheen of the tense skin over the knuckles. He stopped, staring stupidly, and the rage passed from his face, leaving it blank and incredulous.

"Lor' lumme," he muttered. "If that ain't queer."

He held out his hand, palm downwards. And from the pavement I saw that the man's nails were as blue as pieces of turquoise.

The sun came out from behind a passing cloud and sent a sudden flame of radiance over the scene in the side street—the sandwich-board man, his face still blank and incredulous, staring stupidly at his hands; the crowd standing well back in a wide semi-circle; I further forward, peering through my spectacles and clutching my umbrella convulsively. Then a tall man, in morning coat and top-hat, pushed his way through and touched the man from Birmingham on the shoulder.

"Can you come to my house?" he asked in an undertone. "I am a doctor and would like to examine you."

I shifted my gaze and recognized Dr. Symington-Tearle. The man pointed to his boards.

"How about them things?"

"Oh, you can get rid of them. I'll pay you. Here is my card with the address. I'll expect you in half-an-hour, and it will be well worth while your coming."

Symington-Tearle moved away, and a sudden spasm of jealousy affected me as I watched the well-shaped top-hat glittering down the street in the strong sunlight. Why should Symington-Tearle be given an opportunity of impressing a credulous world with some fantastic rubbish of his own devising? I stepped into the road.

"Do you want a five-pound note?" I asked. The man jumped with surprise. "Very well. Come round to this address at once."

I handed him my card. My next move was to telephone to the hospital to say I would be late, and retrace my footsteps homewards.

My visitor arrived in a very short time, after handing over his boards to a comrade on the understanding of suitable compensation, and was shown into my study. Sarakoff was present, and he pored over the man's nails and eyes and skin with rapt attention. At last he enquired how he felt.

"Ain't never felt so well in me life," said the man. "I was saying to a pal this morning 'ow well I felt."

"Do you feel as if you were drunk?" asked Sarakoff tentatively.

"Well, sir, now you put it that way, I feel as if I'd 'ad a good glass of beer. Not drunk, but 'appy."

"Are you naturally cheerful?"

"I carn't say as I am, sir. My profession ain't a very cheery one, not in all sorts and kinds of weather."

"But you are distinctly more cheerful this morning than usual?"

"I am, sir. I don't deny it. I lost my temper sudden like when that crowd drew away from me as if I'd got the leprosy, and I'm usually a mild and forbearin' man."

"Sit down," said Sarakoff. The man obeyed, and Sarakoff began to examine him carefully. He told him once or twice not to speak, but the man seemed in a loquacious mood and was incapable of silence for more than a minute of time.

33

"And I ain't felt so clear 'eaded not for years," he remarked. "I seem to see twice as many things to what I used to, and everything seems to 'ave a new coat of paint. I was saying to a pal early this morning what a very fine place Trafalgar Square was and 'ow I'd never seemed to notice it before, though I've known it all my life. And up Regent Street I begun to notice all sort o' little things I'd never seen before, though it was my old beat 'afore I went to Birmingham. O' course it may be because I been out o' London a spell. But blest if I ever seed so many fine shop windows in Regent Street before, or so many different colours."

"Headache?"

"Bless you, no, sir. Just the opposite, if you understand." He looked round suddenly. "What's that noise?" he asked. "It's been worryin' me since I came in here."

We listened intently, but neither I nor Sarakoff could hear anything.

"It comes from there." The man pointed to the laboratory door. I went and opened it and stood listening. In a corner by the window a clock-work recording barometer was ticking with a faint rhythm.

"That's the noise," said the man from Birmingham. "I knew it wasn't no clock, 'cause it's too fast."

Sarakoff glanced significantly at me.

"All the senses very acute," he said. "At least, hearing and seeing." He took a bottle from the laboratory and uncorked it in one corner of the study. "Can you smell what this is?"

The man, sitting ten feet away, gave one sniff.

"Ammonia," he said promptly, and sneezed. "This 'ere Blue Disease," said the man after a long pause, "is it dangerous?"

He spread out his fingers, squeezing the turquoise nails to see if the colour faded. He frowned to find it fixed. I was standing at the window, my back to the room and my hands twisting nervously with each other behind me.

"No, it is not dangerous," said Sarakoff. He sat on the edge of the writing-table, swinging his legs and staring meditatively at the floor. "It is not dangerous, is it, Harden?"

I replied only with a jerky, impatient movement.

"What I mean," persisted the man, "is this—supposin' the police arrest me, when I go back to my job. 'Ave they a right? 'Ave people a right to give me the shove—to put me in a 'orspital? That crowd round me in the street—it confused me, like—as if I was a leper." He paused and looked up at Sarakoff enquiringly. "What's the cause of it?"

34

"A germ—a bacillus."

"Same as what gives consumption?"

Sarakoff nodded. "But this germ is harmless," he added.

"Then I ain't going to die?"

"No. That's just the point. You aren't going to die," said the Russian slowly. "That's what is so strange."

I jumped round from the window.

"How do you know?" I said fiercely. "There's no proof. It's all theory so far. The calculations may be wrong."

The man stared at me wonderingly. He saw me as a man fighting with some strange anxiety, with his forehead damp and shining, his spectacles aslant on his nose and the heavy folds of his frock-coat shaken with a sudden impetuosity.

"How do you know?" I repeated, shaking my fist in the air. "How do you know he isn't going to die?"

Sarakoff fingered his beard in silence, but his eyes shone with a quiet certainty. To the man from Birmingham it must have seemed suddenly strange that we should behave in this manner. His mind was sharpened to perceive things. Yesterday, had he been present at a similar scene, he would probably have sat dully, finding nothing curious in my passionate attitude and the calm, almost insolent, inscrutability of Sarakoff. He forgot his turquoise finger nails, and stared, open-mouthed.

"Ain't going to die?" he said. "What do yer mean?"

"Simply that you aren't going to die," was Sarakoff's soft answer.

"Yer mean, not die of the Blue Disease?"

"Not die at all."

"Garn! Not die at all." He looked at me. "What's he mean, Mister?" He looked almost surprised with himself at catching the drift of Sarakoff's sentence. Inwardly he felt something insistent and imperious, forcing him to grasp words, to blunder into new meanings. Some new force was alive in him and he was carried on by it in spite of himself. He felt strung up to a pitch of nervous irritation. He got up from his chair and came forward, pointing at Sarakoff. "What's this?" he demanded. "Why don't you speak out? Yer cawn't hide it from me." He stopped. His brain, working at unwonted speed, had discovered a fresh suspicion. "Look 'ere, you two know something about this blue disease." He came a step closer, and looking cunningly in my face, said: "That's why you offered me a five-pound note, ain't it?"

I avoided the scrutiny of the sparrow-egg blue orbs close before me.

"I offered you the money because I wished to examine you," I said shortly. "Here it is. You can go now."

I took a note from a safe in the corner of the room, and held it out. The man took it, felt its crispness and stowed it away in a secure pocket. His thoughts were temporarily diverted by the prospect of an immediate future with plenty of money, and he picked up his hat and went to the door. But his turquoise finger nails lying against the rusty black of the hat brought him back to his suspicions. He paused and turned.

"My name's Wain," he said. "I'm telling you, in case you might 'ear of me again. 'Erbert Wain. I know what yours is, remember, because I seed it on the door." He twisted his hat round several times in his hands and drew his brows together, puzzled at the speed of his ideas. Then he remembered the card that Symington-Tearle had given him.

He pulled it out and examined it. "I'm going across to see this gent," he announced. "It's convenient, 'im living so close. Perhaps he'll 'ave a word to say about this 'ere disease. Fair spread over Birmingham, so they say. It would be nasty if any bloke was responsible for it. Good day to yer." He opened the door slowly, and glanced back at us standing in the middle of the room watching him. "Look 'ere," he said swiftly, "what did 'e mean, saying I was never going to die and——" The light from the window was against his eyes, and he could not see the features of Sarakoff's face, but there was something in the outline of his body that checked him. "Guv'ner, it ain't true." The words came hoarsely from his lips. "I ain't never not going to die."

Sarakoff spoke.

"You are never going to die, Mr. Herbert Wain ... you understand?... Never going to die, unless you get killed in an accident—or starve."

I jerked up my hand to stop my friend.

Wain stared incredulously. Then he burst into a roar of laughter and smacked his thigh.

"Gor lumme!" he exclaimed, "if that ain't rich. Never going to die! Live for ever! Strike me, if that ain't a notion!" The tears ran down his cheeks and he paused to wipe them away. "If I was to believe what you say," he went on, "it would fair drive me crazy. Live for ever—s'elp me, if that wouldn't be just 'ell. Good-day to yer, gents. I'm obliged to yer."

He went out into the sunlit street still roaring with laughter, a thin, ragged, tattered figure, with the shadow of immortality upon him.

CHAPTER X

THE ILLNESS OF MR. ANNOT

The departure of Mr. Herbert Wain was a relief. I turned to Sarakoff at once and spoke with some heat.

"You were more than imprudent to give that fellow hints that we knew more about the Blue Disease than anybody else," I exclaimed. "This may be the beginning of incalculable trouble."

"Nonsense," replied the Russian. "You are far too apprehensive, Harden. What can he do?"

"What may he not do?" I cried bitterly. "Do you suppose London will welcome the spread of the germ? Do you think that people will be pleased to know that you and I were responsible for its appearance?"

"When they realize that it brings immortality with it, they will hail us as the saviours of humanity."

"Mr. Herbert Wain did not seem to accept the idea of immortality with any pleasure," I muttered. "The suggestion seemed to strike him as terrible."

Sarakoff laughed genially.

"My friend," he said, "Mr. Herbert Wain is not a man of vision. He is a cockney, brought up in the streets of a callous city. To him life is a hard struggle, and immortality naturally appears in a poor light. You must have patience. It will take some time before the significance of this immortality is grasped by the people. But when it is grasped, all the conditions of life will change. Life will become beautiful. We will have reforms that, under ordinary circumstances, would have taken countless ages to bring about. We will anticipate our evolution by thousands of centuries. At one step we will reach the ultimate goal of our destiny."

"And what is that?"

"Immortality, of course. Surely you must see by now that all the activities of modern life are really directed towards one end— towards solving the riddle of prolonging life and at the same time increasing pleasure? Isn't that the inner secret desire that you doctors find in every patient? So far a compromise has only been possible, but now that is all changed."

"I don't agree, Sarakoff. Some people must live for other motives. Take myself ... I live for science."

37

"It is merely your form of pleasure."

"That's a quibble," I cried angrily. "Science is aspiration. There's all the difference in the world between aspiration and pleasure. I have scarcely known what pleasure is. I have worked like a slave all my life, with the sole ambition of leaving something permanent behind me when I die."

"But you won't die," interposed the Russian. "That is the charm of the new situation."

"Then why should I work?" The question shaped itself in my mind and I uttered it involuntarily. I sat down and stared at the fire. A kind of dull depression came over me, and for some reason the picture of Sarakoff's butterflies appeared in my mind. I saw them with great distinctness, crawling aimlessly on the floor of their cage. "Why should I work?" I repeated.

Sarakoff merely shrugged his shoulders and turned away. Questions of that kind did not seem to bother him. His was a nature that escaped the necessity of self-analysis. But I was different, and our conversation had aroused a train of odd thought. What, after all, was it that kept my nose to the grindstone? Why had I slaved incessantly all my life, reading when I might have slept, examining patients when I might have been strolling through meadows, hurrying through meals when I might have eaten at leisure? What was the cause behind all the tremendous activity and feverish haste of modern people? When Sarakoff had said that I would not die, and that therein lay the charm of the new situation, it seemed as if scales had momentarily fallen from my eyes. I beheld myself as something ridiculous, comparable to a hare that persists in dashing along a country lane in front of the headlight of a motor car, when a turn one way or another would bring it to safety. A great uneasiness filled me, and with it came a determination to ignore these new fields of thought that loomed round me—a determination that I have seen in old men when they are faced by the new and contradictory—and I began to force my attention elsewhere. I was relieved when the door opened and my servant entered. She handed me a telegram. It was from Miss Annot, asking me to come to Cambridge at once, as her father was seriously ill. I scribbled a reply, saying I would be down that afternoon.

After the servant had left the room, I remained gazing at the fire, but my depression left me. In place of it I felt a quiet elation, and it was not difficult for me to account for it.

"I was wrong in saying that I had scarcely known what pleasure is," I observed at length, looking up at Sarakoff with a

38

smile. "I must confess to you that there is one factor in my life that gives me great pleasure."

Sarakoff placed himself before me, hands in pockets and pipe in mouth, and gazed at me with an answering smile in his dark face.

"A woman?"

I flushed. The Russian seemed amused.

"I thought as much," he remarked. "This year I noticed a change in you. Your fits of abstraction suggested it. Well, may I congratulate you? When are you to be married?"

"That is out of the question at present," I answered hurriedly. "In fact, there is no definite arrangement—just a mutual understanding.... She is not free."

Sarakoff raised his shaggy eyebrows.

"Then she is already married?"

This cross-examination was intensely painful to me. Between Miss Annot and myself there was, I hoped, a perfect understanding, and I quite realized the girl's position. She was devoted to her father, who required her constant attention and care, and until she was free there could be no question of marriage, or even an engagement, for fear of wounding the old man's feelings. I quite appreciated her situation and was content to wait.

"No! She has an invalid father, and——"

"Rubbish!" said Sarakoff, with remarkable force. "Rubbish! Marry her, man, and then think of her father. Why, that sort of thing——" He drew a deep breath and checked himself.

I shook my head.

"That is impossible. Here, in England, we cannot do such things.... The girl's duty is plain. I am quite prepared to wait."

"To wait for what?"

I looked at him in unthinking surprise.

"Until Mr. Annot dies, of course."

Sarakoff remained motionless. Then he took his pipe out of his mouth, strolled to the window, and began to whistle to himself in subdued tones. A moment later he left the room. I picked up a time-table and looked out a train, a little puzzled by his behaviour.

I reached Cambridge early in the afternoon and took a taxi to the Annots' house. Miss Annot met me at the door.

"It is so good of you to come," she said with a faint smile. "My father behaved very foolishly yesterday. He insisted on inviting the Perrys to lunch, and he talked a great deal and insisted on drinking wine, with the result that in the night he had a return of his gastritis. He is very weak to-day and his mind seems to be wandering a little."

39

"You should not have allowed him to do that," I remonstrated. "He is in too fragile a state to run any risks."

"Oh, but I couldn't help it. The Perrys are such old friends of father's, and they were only staying one day in Cambridge. Father would have fretted if they had not come."

I had taken off my coat in the hall, and we were now standing in the drawing-room.

"You are tired, Alice," I said.

"I've been up most of the night," she replied, with an effort towards brightness. "But I do feel tired, I admit."

I turned away from her and went to the window. For the first time I felt the awkwardness of our position. I had a strong and natural impulse to comfort her, but what could I do? After a moment's reflection, I made a sudden resolution.

"Alice," I said, "you and I had better become engaged. Don't you think it would be easier for you?"

"Oh, don't," she cried. "Father would never endure the idea that I belonged to another man. He would worry about my leaving him continually. No, please wait. Perhaps it will not be——"

She checked herself. I remained silent, staring at the pattern of the carpet with a frown. To my annoyance, I could not keep Sarakoff's words out of my mind. And yet Alice was right. I felt sure that no one is a free agent in the sense that he or she can be guided solely by love. It is necessary to make a compromise. As these thoughts formed in my mind I again seemed to hear the loud voice of Sarakoff, sounding in derision at my cautious views. A conflict arose in my soul. I raised my eyes and looked at Alice. She was standing by the mantelpiece, staring listlessly at the grate. A wave of emotion passed over me. I took a step towards her.

"Alice!" And then the words stuck in my throat. She turned her head and her eyes questioned me. I tried to continue, but something prevented me, and I became suddenly calm again. "Please take me up to your father," I begged her. She obeyed silently, and I followed her upstairs.

Mr. Annot was lying in a darkened room with his eyes closed. He was a very old man, approaching ninety, with a thin aquiline face and white hair. He lay very still, and at first I thought he was unconscious. But his pulse was surprisingly good, and his breathing deep and regular.

"He is sleeping," I murmured.

She leaned over the bed.

"He scarcely slept during the night," she whispered. "This will do him good."

"His pulse could not be better," I murmured.

She peered at him more closely.

"Isn't he very pale?"

I stooped down, so that my face was close to hers. The old man certainly looked very pale. A marble-like hue lay over his features, and yet the skin was warm to the touch.

"How long has he been asleep?" I asked.

"He was awake over an hour ago, when I looked in last. He said then that he was feeling drowsy."

"I think we'll wake him up."

Alice hesitated.

"Won't you wait for tea?" she whispered. "He would probably be awake by then."

I shook my head.

"I must get back to London by five. Do you mind if we have a little more light?"

She moved to the window and raised the blind half way. I examined the old man attentively. There was no doubt about the curious pallor of his skin. It was like the pallor of extreme collapse, save for the presence of a faint colour in his cheeks which seemed to lie as a bright transparency over a dead background. My fingers again sought his pulse. It was full and steady. As I counted it my eyes rested on his hand.

I stooped down suddenly with an exclamation. Alice hurried to my side.

"Where did those friends of his come from?" I asked swiftly.

"The Perrys? From Birmingham."

"Was there anything wrong with them?"

"What do you mean?"

Before I could reply the old man opened his eyes. The light fell clearly on his face. Alice uttered a cry of horror. I experienced an extraordinary sensation of fear. Out of the marble pallor of Mr. Annot's face, two eyes, stained a sparrow-egg blue, stared keenly at us.

41

CHAPTER XI

THE RESURRECTION

For some moments none of us spoke. Alice recovered herself first.

"What is the matter with him?" she gasped.

I was incapable of finding a suitable reply, and stood, tongue-tied, staring foolishly at the old man. He seemed a little surprised at our behaviour.

"Dr. Harden," he said, "I am glad to see you. My daughter did not tell me you were coming."

His voice startled me. It was strong and clear. On my previous visit to him he had spoken in quavering tones.

"Oh, father, how do you feel?" exclaimed Alice, kneeling beside the bed.

"My dear, I feel extremely well. I have not felt so well for many years." He stretched out his hand and patted his daughter's head. "Yes, my sleep has done me good. I should like to get up for tea."

"But your eyes——" stammered Alice "Can you see, father?"

"See, my dear? What does she mean, Dr. Harden?"

"There is some discolouration of the conjunctivæ," I said hastily. "It is nothing to worry about."

At that moment Alice caught sight of his finger nails.

"Look!" she cried, "they're blue."

The old man raised his hands and looked at them in astonishment.

"How extraordinary," he murmured. "What do you make of that, doctor?"

"It is nothing," I assured him. "It is only pigmentation caused—er—caused by some harmless germ."

"I know what it is," cried Alice suddenly. "It's the Blue Disease. Father, you remember the Perrys were telling us about it yesterday at lunch. They said it was all over Birmingham, and that they had come south partly to escape it. They must have brought the infection with them."

"Yes," I said, "that is certainly the explanation. And now, Mr. Annot, let me assure you that this disease is harmless. It has no ill effects."

42

Mr. Annot sat up in bed with an exhibition of vigour that was remarkable in a man of his age.

"I can certainly witness to the fact that it causes no ill effects, Dr. Harden," he exclaimed. "This morning I felt extremely weak and was prepared for the end. But now I seem to have been endowed with a fresh lease of life. I feel young again. Do you think this Blue Disease is the cause of it?"

"Possibly. It is difficult to say," I answered in some confusion. "But you must not think of getting up, Mr. Annot. Rest in bed for the next week is essential."

"Humbug!" cried the old man, fixing his brilliant eyes upon me. "I am going to get up this instant."

"Oh, father, please don't be so foolish!"

"Foolish, child? Do you think I'm going to lie here when I feel as if my body and mind had been completely rejuvenated? I repeat I am going to get up. Nothing on earth will keep me in bed."

The old man began to remove the bedclothes. I made an attempt to restrain him, but was met by an outburst of irritation that warned me not to interfere. I motioned Alice to follow me, and together we left the room. As we went downstairs I heard a curious sound proceeding from Mr. Annot's bedroom. We halted on the stairs and listened. The sound became louder and clearer.

"Father is singing," said Alice in a low voice. Then she took out her handkerchief and began to sob.

We continued our way downstairs, Alice endeavouring to stifle her sobs, and I in a dazed condition of mind. I was stunned by the fact that that mad experiment of ours should have had such a sudden and strange result. It produced in me a fear that was far worse to bear than the vague anxiety I had felt ever since those fatal tubes of the Sarakoff-Harden bacillus had been emptied into the lake. I stumbled into the drawing-room and threw myself upon a chair. My legs were weak, and my hands were trembling.

"Alice," I said, "you must not allow this to distress you. The Blue Disease is not dangerous."

She lifted a tear-stained face and looked at me dully.

"Richard, I can't bear it any longer. I've given half my life to looking after father. I simply can't bear it."

I sat up and stared at her. What strange intuition had come to her?

"What do you mean?"

She sobbed afresh.

"I can't endure the sight of him with those blue eyes," she went on, rather wildly. "Richard, I must get away. I've never been from him for more than a few hours at a time for the last fifteen years. Don't think I want him to die."

"I don't."

"I'm glad he's better," she remarked irrelevantly.

"So am I."

"The Perrys were saying that the doctors up in Birmingham think that the Blue Disease cut short other diseases, and made people feel better." She twisted her handkerchief for some moments. "Does it?" she asked, looking at me directly.

"I—er—I have heard it does."

An idea had come into my mind, and I could not get rid of it. Why should I not tell her all that I knew?

"I'm thirty-five," she remarked.

"And I'm forty-two." I tried to smile.

"Life's getting on for us both," she added.

"I know, Alice. I suggested that we should get engaged a short while ago. Now I suggest that we get married—as soon as possible." I got up and paced the room. "Why not?" I demanded passionately.

She shook her head, and appeared confused.

"It's impossible. Who could look after him? I should never be happy, Richard, as long as he was living."

I stopped before her.

"Not with me?"

"No, Richard. I should be left a great deal to myself. A doctor's wife always is. I've thought it out carefully. I would think of him."

After a long silence, I made a proposal that I had refused to entertain before.

"Well, there's no reason why he should not come and live with us. There is plenty of room in my house at Harley Street. Would that do?"

It was a relief to me when she said that she would not consent to an arrangement of that kind. I sat down again.

"Alice," I said quietly, "it is necessary that we should decide our future. There are special reasons."

She glanced at me enquiringly. There was a pause in which I tried to collect my thoughts.

"Your father," I continued, "is suffering from a very peculiar disease. It is wrong, perhaps, to call it a disease. You wouldn't call life a disease, would you?"

"I don't understand."

"No, of course not. Well, to put it as simply as possible, it is likely that your father will live a long time now. When he said he felt as if his mind and body had been rejuvenated he was speaking the truth."

"But he will be ninety next year," she said bluntly.

"I know. But that will make no difference. This germ, that is now in his body, has the power of arresting all further decay. Your father will remain as he is now for an indefinite period."

I met her eyes as steadily as I could, but there was a quality in her gaze that caused me to look elsewhere.

"How do you know this?" she asked after a painful silence.

"I—er—I can't tell you." The colour mounted to my cheeks, and I began to tap the carpet impatiently with the toe of my boot. "You wouldn't understand," I continued in as professional a manner as I could muster. "You would need first to study the factors that bring about old age."

"Where did the Blue Disease come from? Tell me. I can surely understand that!"

"You have read the paper, haven't you?"

"I've read that no one understands what it is, and that the doctors are puzzled."

"How should I know where it comes from?"

She regarded me searchingly.

"You know something about it," she said positively. "Richard, you are keeping it back from me. I have a right to know what it is."

I was silent.

"If you don't tell me, how can I trust you again?" she asked. "Don't you see that there will always be a shadow between us?"

It was not difficult for me to guess that my guilty manner had roused her suspicions. She had seen my agitation, and had found it unaccountable. I resolved to entrust her with the secret of the germ.

"Do you remember that I once told you my friend, Professor Sarakoff, had succeeded in keeping butterflies alive for over a year?"

She nodded.

"He and I have been experimenting on those lines and he has found a germ that has the property of keeping human beings alive in the same way. The germ has escaped ... into the world ... and it is the cause of the Blue Disease."

"How did it escape?"

I winced. In her voice I was conscious of a terrible accusation.

"By accident," I stammered.

She jumped to her feet.

"I don't believe it! That is a lie!"

"Alice, you must calm yourself! I am trying to tell you exactly what happened."

45

"Was it by accident?"

The vision of that secret expedition to the water supply of Birmingham passed before me. I felt like a criminal. I could not raise my eyes; my cheeks were burning. In the silence that followed, the sound of Mr. Annot's voice became audible. Alice stood before me, rigid and implacable.

"It was—by accident," I said. I tried to look at her, and failed. She remained motionless for about a minute. Then she turned and left the room. I heard her go slowly upstairs. A door banged. Actuated by a sudden desire, I stepped into the hall, seized my coat and hat and opened the front door. I was just in time. As I gently closed the door I heard Mr. Annot on the landing above. He was singing some long-forgotten tune in a strange cracked voice.

I stood outside on the doorstep, listening, until, overcome by curiosity, I bent down and lifted the flap of the letter-box. The interior of the hall was plainly visible. Mr. Annot had ceased singing and was now standing before the mirror which hung beside the hatstand. He was a trifle unsteady, and swayed on his frail legs, but he was staring at himself with a kind of savage intensity. At last he turned away and I caught the expression on his face.... With a slight shiver, I let down the flap noiselessly.There was something in that expression that for me remains unnamable; and I think now, as I look back into those past times, that of all the signs which showed me that the Sarakoff-Harden bacillus was an offence against humanity, that strange look on the nonagenarian's face was the most terrible and obvious.

CHAPTER XII

MR. CLUTTERBUCK'S OPINION

When I reached London it was dusk, and a light mist hung in the darkening air. The lamps were twinkling in the streets. I decided to get some tea in a restaurant adjoining the station. When I entered it was crowded, and the only seat that was empty was at a small table already occupied by another man. I sat down, and gave my order to the waitress, and remained staring moodily at the soiled marble surface of the table. My neighbour was engrossed in his paper.

During my journey from Cambridge I had come to a certain conclusion. Sarakoff was of the opinion that we should publish a statement about the germ of immortality, and now I was in agreement with him. For I had been reflecting upon the capacity of human mind for retaining secrets and had come to the conclusion that it is so constructed that its power of retention is remarkably small. I felt that it would be a matter of extraordinary relief if everyone in that tea-shop knew the secret of the Blue Germ.

I began to study the man who sat opposite me. He was a quietly dressed middle-aged man. The expression on his rather pale, clean-shaven face suggested that he was a clerk or secretary. He looked reliable, unimaginative, careful and methodical. He was reading his newspaper with close attention. A cup of tea and the remains of a toasted muffin were at his elbow. It struck me that here was a very average type of man, and an immense desire seized upon me to find out what opinion he would pronounce if I were to tell him my secret. I waited until he looked up.

"Is there any news?" I asked.

He observed me for a moment as if he resented my question.

"The Blue Disease is spreading in London," he remarked shortly, and returned to his paper. I felt rebuffed, but reflected that this, after all, was how an average man might be expected to behave.

"A curious business," I continued. "I am a doctor, and therefore very much interested in it."

His manner changed. He assumed the attitude of the average man towards a doctor at once, and I was gratified to observe it.

"I was just thinking I'd like to hear what a doctor thinks about it," he said, laying down his paper. "I thought of calling in on Dr.

47

Sykes on my way home to-night; he attends my wife. Do you know Dr. Sykes?"

"Which one?" I asked cautiously, not willing to disappoint him.

"Dr. Sykes of Harlesden," he said, with a look of surprise.

"Oh, yes, I know Dr. Sykes. Why did you think of going to see him?"

He smiled apologetically and pointed to the paper.

"It sounds so queer ... the disease. They say, up in Birmingham, that it's stopping all diseases in the hospitals ... everywhere. People getting well all of a sudden. Now I don't believe that."

"Have you seen a case yet?"

"Yes. A woman. In the street this afternoon as I was coming from lunch. The police took her. She was mad, I can tell you. There was a big crowd. She screamed. I think she was drunk." He paused, and glanced at me. "What do you think of it?"

I took a deep breath.

"I don't think, I know," I said, in as quiet a manner as possible. He stared a moment, and a nervous smile appeared and swiftly vanished. He seemed uncertain what to do.

"You've found out something?" he asked at length, playing with his teaspoon and keeping his eyes on the table. I regarded him carefully. I was not quite certain if he still thought I was a doctor.

"I'm not a lunatic," I said. "I'm merely stating a rather extraordinary fact. I know all about the germ of the Blue Disease."

He raised his eyes for an instant, and then lowered them. His hand had stopped trifling with the teaspoon.

"Yes," he said, "the doctors think it's due to a germ of some sort." He made a sort of effort and continued. "It is funny, some of these germs being invisible through microscopes. Measles and chickenpox and common things like that. They've never seen the germs that cause them, that's what the papers say. It seems odd—having something you can't see." He turned his head, and looked for his hat that hung on a peg behind him.

"One moment," I said. I took out my card-case. "I want you to read this card. Don't think I'm mad. I want to talk to you for a particular reason which I'll explain in a moment." He took the card hesitatingly and read it. Then he looked at me. "The reason why I am speaking to you is this," I said. "I want to find out what a decent citizen like yourself will think of something I know. It concerns the Blue Disease and its origin."

He seemed disturbed, and took out his watch.

48

"I ought to get home. My wife——"

"Is your wife ill?"

"Yes."

"What's the matter with her?"

He frowned.

"Dr. Sykes thinks it's lung trouble."

"Consumption?"

He nodded, and an expression of anxiety came over his face.

"Good," I exclaimed. "Now listen to what I have to say. Before the week is out your wife will be cured. I swear it."

He said nothing. It was plain that he was still suspicious.

"You read what they say in the papers about the Blue Disease cutting short other diseases? Well, that Blue Disease will be all over London in a day or two. Now do you understand?"

I saw that I had interested him. He settled himself on his chair, and began to examine me. His gaze travelled over my face and clothes, pausing at my cuff-links and my tie and collar. Then he looked at my card again. Inwardly he came to a decision.

"I'm willing to listen to what you've got to say," he remarked, "if you think it's worth saying."

"Thank you. I think it's worth hearing." I leaned my arms on the table in front of me. "This Blue Disease is not an accidental thing. It was deliberately planned, by two scientists. I was one of those scientists."

"You can't plan a disease," he remarked, after a considerable silence.

"You're wrong. We found a way of creating new germs. We worked at the idea of creating a particular kind of germ that would kill all other germs ... and we were successful. Then we let loose the germ on the world."

"How?"

"We infected the water supply of Birmingham at its origin in Wales."

I watched his expression intently.

"You mean that you did this secretly, without knowing what the result would be?" he asked at last.

"We foresaw the result to a certain extent."

He thought for some time.

"But you had no right to infect a water supply. That's criminal, surely?"

"It's criminal if the infection is dangerous to people. If you put cholera in a reservoir, of course it's criminal."

"But this germ...?"

49

"This germ does not kill people. It kills the germs in people."

"What's the difference?"

"All the difference in the world! It's like this.... By the way, what is your name?"

"Clutterbuck." The word escaped his lips by accident. He looked annoyed. I smiled reassuringly.

"It's like this, Mr. Clutterbuck. If you kill all the germs in a person's body, that person doesn't die. He lives ... indefinitely. Now do you see?"

"No, I don't see," said Clutterbuck with great frankness. "I don't understand what you're driving at. You tell me that you're a doctor and you give me a card bearing a well-known specialist's name. Then you say you created a germ and put it in the Birmingham water supply and that the result is the Blue Disease. This germ, you say, doesn't kill people, but does something else which I don't follow. Now I was taught that germs are dangerous things, and it seems to me that if your story is true—which I don't believe—you are guilty of a criminal act." He pushed back his chair and reached for his hat. There was a flush on his face.

"Then you don't believe my tale?"

"No, I'm sorry, but I don't."

"Well, Mr. Clutterbuck, will you believe it when you see your wife restored to health in a few days' time?"

He paused and stared at me.

"What you say is impossible," he said slowly. "If you were a doctor you'd know that as well as I do."

"But the reports in the paper?"

"Oh, that's journalistic rubbish."

He picked up his umbrella and beckoned to the waitress. I made a last attempt.

"If I take you to my house will you believe me then?"

"Look here," he said in an angry tone, "I've had enough of this. I can't waste my time. I'm sure of one thing and that is that you're no doctor. You've got somebody's card-case. You don't look like a doctor and you don't speak like one. I should advise you to be careful."

He moved away from the table. Some neighbouring people stared at me for a moment and then went on eating. Mr. Clutterbuck paid at the desk and left the establishment. I had received the verdict of the average man.

CHAPTER XIII

THE DEAD IMMORTAL

When I reached home, Sarakoff was out. He had left a message to say he would not be in until after midnight, as he was going to hear Leonora sing at the opera, and purposed to take her to supper afterwards. Dinner was therefore a solitary meal for me, and when it was all over I endeavoured to plunge into some medical literature. The hours passed slowly. It was almost impossible to read, for the process, to me, was similar to trying to take an interest in a week-old newspaper.

The thought of the bacillus made the pages seem colourless; it dwarfed all meaning in the words. I gave up the attempt and set myself to smoking and gazing into the fire. What was I to do about Alice?

Midnight came and my mind was still seething. I knew sleep was out of the question and the desire to walk assailed me. I put on a coat and hat and left the house. It was a cold night, clear with stars. Harley Street was silent. My footsteps led me south towards the river. I walked rapidly, oblivious of others. The problem of Alice was beyond solution, for the simple reason that I found it impossible to think of her clearly. She was overshadowed by the wonder of the bacillus. But the picture of her father haunted me. It filled me with strange emotions, and at moments with stranger misgivings.

There are meanings, dimly caught at the time, which remain in the mind like blind creatures, mewing and half alive. They pluck at the brain ceaselessly, seeking birth in thought. Old Annot's face peering into the hall mirror—what was it that photographed the scene so pitilessly in my memory? I hurried along, scarcely noticing where I went, and as I went I argued with myself aloud.

On the Embankment I returned to a full sense of my position in space. The river ran beneath me, cold and dark. I leaned over the stone balustrade and stared at the dark forms of barges. Yes, it was true enough that I had not realized that the germ would keep Mr. Annot alive indefinitely. Sarakoff's significant whistle that morning came to my mind, and I saw that I had been guilty of singular denseness in not understanding its meaning.

And now old Annot would live on and on, year after year. Was

I glad? It is impossible to say. It was that expression in the old man's face that dominated me. I tried to think it out. It had been a triumphant look; and more than that ... a triumphant toothless look. Was that the solution? I reflected that triumph is an expression that belongs to youth, to young things, to all that is striving upwards in growth. Surely old people should look only patient and resigned—never triumphant—in this world? Some strong action with regard to Alice's position would be necessary. It was absurd to think that her father should eternally come between her and me. It would be necessary to go down to Cambridge and make a clean confession to Alice. And then, when forgiven, I would insist on an immediate arrangement concerning our marriage. Marriage! The word vibrated in my soul. The solemnity of that ceremony was great enough to mere mortals, but what would it mean to us when we were immortals? Sarakoff had hinted at a new marriage system. Was such a thing possible? On what factors did marriage rest? Was it merely a discipline or was it ultimately selfishness?

My agitation increased, and I hurried eastwards, soon entering an area of riverside London that, had I been calmer, might have given me some alarm. It must have been about two o'clock in the morning when the pressure of thoughts relaxed in my mind. I found myself in the great dock area. The forms of giant cranes rose dimly in the air. A distant glare of light, where nightshifts were at work, illuminated the huge shapes of ocean steamers. The quays were littered with crates and bales. A clanking of buffers and the shrill whistles of locomotives came out of the darkness. For some time I stood transfixed. In my imagination I saw these big ships, laden with cargo, slipping down the Thames and out into the sea, carrying with them an added cargo to every part of the earth. For by them would the Blue Germ travel over the waterways of the world and enter every port. From the ports it would spread swiftly into the towns, and from the towns onwards across plain and prairie until the gift of Immortality had been received by every human being. The vision thrilled me....

A commotion down a side street on my right shattered this glorious picture. Hoarse cries rang out, and a sound of blows. I could make out a small dark struggling mass which seemed to break into separate parts and then coalesce again. A police whistle sounded. The mass again broke up, and some figures came rushing down the street in my direction. They passed me in a flash, and vanished. At the far end of the street two twinkling lights appeared. After a period of hesitation—what doctor goes willingly into the accidents of the streets?—I walked slowly in their direction.

When I reached them I found two policemen bending over the body of a man, which lay in the gutter face downwards.

"Good evening," I said. "Can I be of any service? I am a doctor."

They shone their lamps on me suspiciously. "What are you doing here?"

"Walking," I replied. Exercise had calmed me. I felt cool and collected. "I often walk far at nights. Let me see the body."

I stooped down and turned the body over. The policemen watched me in silence. The body was that of a young, fair-haired sailor man. There was a knife between his ribs. His eyes were screwed up into a rigid state of contraction which death had not yet relaxed. His whole body was rigid. I knew that the knife had pierced his heart. But the most extraordinary thing about him was his expression. I have never looked on a face either in life or death that expressed such terror. Even the policemen were startled. The light of their lamps shone on that monstrous and distorted countenance, and we gazed in horrified silence.

"Is he dead?" asked one at last.

"Quite dead," I replied, "but it is odd to find this rigidity so early." I began to press his eyelids apart. The right eye opened. I uttered a cry of astonishment.

"Look!" I cried.

They stared.

"Blest if that ain't queer," said one. "It's that Blue Disease. He must 'ave come from Birmingham."

"Queer?" I said passionately. "Why, man, it's tragedy— unadulterated tragedy. The man was an Immortal."

They stared at me heavily.

"Immortal?" said one.

"He would have lived for ever," I said. "In his system there is the most marvellous germ that the world has ever known. It was circulating in his blood. It had penetrated to every part of his body. A few minutes ago, as he walked along the dark street, he had before him a future of unnumbered years. And now he lies in the gutter. Can you imagine a greater tragedy?"

The policemen transferred their gaze from me to the dead man. Then, as if moved by a common impulse, they began to laugh. I watched them moodily, plunged in an extraordinary vein of thought. When I moved away they at once stopped me.

"No, you don't," said one. "We'll want you at the police station to give your evidence. Not," he continued with a grin, "to tell that bit

53

of information you just gave us, about him being an angel or something."

"I didn't say he was an angel."

They laughed tolerantly. Like Mr. Clutterbuck, they thought I was mad.

"Let's hope he's an angel," said the other. "But, by his face, he looks more like the other thing. Bill, you go round for the ambulance. I'll stay with the gentleman."

The policeman moved away ponderously and vanished in the darkness.

"What was that you were saying, sir?" asked the policeman who remained with me.

"Never mind," I muttered, "you wouldn't understand."

"I'm interested in religious matters," continued the policeman in a soft voice. "You think that the Blue Disease is something out of the common?"

I am never surprised at London policemen, but I looked at this one closely before I replied.

"You seem a reasonable man," I said. "Let me tell you that what I have told you about the germ—that it confers immortality—is correct. In a day or two you will be immortal."

He seemed to reflect in a calm massive way on the news. His eyes were fixed on the dead man's face.

"An Immortal Policeman?"

"Yes."

"You're asking me to believe a lot, sir."

"I know that. But still, there it is. It's the truth."

"And what about crime?" he continued. "If we were all Immortals, what about crime?"

"Crime will become so horrible in its meaning that it will stop."

"It hasn't stopped yet...."

"Of course not. It won't, till people realize they are immortal."

He shifted his lantern and shone it down the road.

"Well, sir, it seems to me it will be a long time before people realize that. In fact, I don't see how anyone could ever realize it."

"Why not?"

"Just think," he said, with a large air. "Supposing crime died out, what would happen to the Sunday papers? Where would those lawyers be? What would we do with policemen? No, you can't realize it. You can't realize the things you exist for all vanishing. It's not human nature." He brooded for a time. "You can't do away with crime," he continued. "What's behind crime? Woman and gold—one

54

or the other, or both. Now you don't mean to tell me, sir, that the Blue Disease is doing away with women and gold in a place like Birmingham? Why, sir, what made Birmingham? What do you suppose life is?"

"I have never been asked the question before by a policeman," I said. "I do not know what made Birmingham, but I will tell you what life is. It is ultimately a cell, containing protoplasm and a nucleus."

A low rumbling noise began somewhere in his vast bulk. It gradually increased to a roar. I became aware that he was laughing. He held his sides. I thought his shining belt would burst. At length his hilarity slowly subsided, and he became sober. He surveyed the dead body at his feet.

"No, sir," he said, "don't you believe it. Life is women and gold. It always was that, and it always will be." He shone his lamp downwards so that the light fell on the terriblefeatures of the dead sailor. "Now this man, sir, was killed because of money, I'll wager. And behind the money I reckon you'll find a woman." He mused for a time. "Not necessarily a pretty woman, but a woman of some sort."

"How do you account for that look of fear on his face?"

"I couldn't say. I've never seen anything like it. I've seen a lot of dead faces, but they are usually quiet enough, as if they were asleep. But I'll tell you one thing, sir, that I have noticed, and that is that money—which includes diamonds and such like, makes a man die worse and more bitter than anything else."

He turned his lantern down the street. A sound of wheels reached us.

"That's the ambulance."

"Will you really require me at the police station?" I asked.

"Yes."

"Will it be necessary to prove who I am?"

He smiled.

"You won't need to prove that you're a doctor, sir," he said genially. "We have a lot to do with doctors. I could tell you were a doctor after talking a minute with you. You are all the same."

"What do you mean?"

"Well—it's the things you say. Now only a doctor could have said what you did—about life being a cell. Do you know, sir, I sometimes believe that doctors is more innocent than parsons. It's the things they say...."

The low rumbling began again in his interior. I waited silently until the ambulance came up. I felt a slight shade of annoyance. But how could I expect the enormous uneducated bulk beside me to take a really intelligent and scientific view of life? Of course life was a cell. Every educated person knew that—and now that cell was, for the first time in history, about to become immortal—but what did the policeman care? How stupid people were, I reflected. We moved off in a small procession towards the police station. Half an hour later I was on my way west, deeply pondering on the causes of that extraordinary expression of fear in the dead sailor's face. Never in my life before had I seen so agonized a countenance, but I was destined to see others as terrible. As I walked, the strangeness of the dead man's tragedy grew in my mind and filled me with a tremendous wonder, for who had ever seen a dead Immortal?

On reaching home I roused Sarakoff and related to him what I had seen.

CHAPTER XIV

FIRST IMPRESSIONS OF IMMORTALITY

After two hours of sleep I awoke. My brief rest had been haunted by unpleasant dreams, vague and indefinite, but seeming to centre about the idea of an impending catastrophe. I lay in bed staring at the dimly outlined window. I felt quite rested and very wide awake. For some time I remained motionless, reflecting on my night adventures and idly thinking whether it was worth while getting up and attending to some correspondence that was overdue. The prospect of a chilly study was not attractive. And then I noticed a very peculiar sensation.

There is only one thing that I can compare it with. After a day of exhausting work a glass of champagne produces in me an almost immediate effect. I feel as if the worries of the day are suddenly removed to a great and blessed distance. A happy indifference takes their place. I felt the same effect as I lay in bed on that dreary winter's morning. The idea that I should get up and work retreated swiftly. A pleasant sense of languor came over me. My eyes closed and for some time I lay in a blissful state of peace, such as I had never experienced before so far as my memory could tell.

I do not know how long I lay in this state, but at length a persistent noise made me open my eyes. I looked round. It seemed to be full daylight now. The first thing I noticed was the unusual size of the room. The ceiling seemed far above my head. The walls seemed to have receded many feet. In my astonishment I uttered an exclamation. The result was startling. My voice seemed to reverberate and re-echo as if I had shouted with all my strength. Considerably startled, I remained in a sitting posture, gazing at my unfamiliar surroundings. The persistent noise that had first roused me continued, and for a long time I could not account for it. It appeared to come from under my bed. I leaned over the edge, but could see nothing. And then, in a flash, I knew what it was. It was the sound of my watch, that lay under my pillow.

I drew it out and stared at it in a state of mystification. Each of its ticks sounded like a small hammer striking sharply against a metal plate. I held it to my ear and was almost deafened. For a moment I wondered whether I were not in the throes of some acute nervous disorder, in which the senses became sharpened to an incredible degree. Such an exultation of perception could only be due to some powerful intoxicant at work on my body. Was I going mad? I laid the watch on the counterpane and in the act of doing it, the explanation burst on my mind. For the recollection of Mr. Herbert Wain and the Clockdrum suddenly came to me. I flung aside the bedclothes, ran to the window and drew the curtains. The radiance of the day almost blinded me. I pressed my hands to my eyes in a kind of agony, feeling that they had been seared and destroyed, and dropped on my knees. I remained in this position for over a minute and then gradually withdrew my hands and gazed at the carpet. I dared not look up yet. The pattern of the carpet glowed in colours more brilliant than I had ever seen before. As I knelt there, in attitude of prayer, it seemed to me that I had never noticed colour before; that all my life had been passed without any consciousness of colour. At last I lifted my sight from the miracle of the carpet to the miracle of the day. High overhead, through the dingy windowpane, was a patch of clear sky, infinitely sweet, remote and inaccessible, framed by golden clouds. As I gazed at it an indescribable reverence and joy filled my mind. In the purity of the morning light, it seemed the most lovely and wonderful thing I had ever beheld. And I, Richard Harden, consulting physician who had hitherto looked on life through a microscope, remained kneeling on my miraculous carpet, gazing upwards at the miraculous heavens. Acting on some strange impulse I stretched out my hands, and then I saw something which turned me into a rigid statue.

It was in this attitude that Sarakoff found me.

He entered my room violently. His hair was tousled and his beard stuck out at a grotesque angle. He was clad in pink pyjamas, and in his hand he carried a silver-backed mirror. My attitude did not seem to cause him any surprise. The door slammed behind him, with a noise of thunder, and he rushed across the room to where I knelt, and stooping, examined my finger nails at which I was staring.

"Good!" he shouted. "Good! Harden, you've got it too!"

He pointed triumphantly. Under the nails there was a faint tinge of blue, and at the nail-bed this was already intense, forming little crescent-shaped areas of vivid turquoise.

Sarakoff sat down on the edge of my bed and studied himself attentively in the hand mirror.

"A slight pallor is perceptible in the skin," he announced as if he was dictating a note for a medical journal, "and this is due, no doubt, to a deposit of the blue pigment in the deeper layers of the epidermis. The hair is at present unaffected save at the roots. God knows what colour blond hair will become. I am anxious about Leonora. The expression—I suppose I can regard myself as a typical case, Harden—is serene, if not animated. Subjectively, one may observe a great sense of exhilaration coupled with an extraordinary increase in the power of perception. You, for example, look to me quite different."

"In what way?" I demanded.

"Well, as you kneel there, I notice in you a kind of angular grandeur, a grotesque touch of the sublime, that was not evident to me before. If I were a sculptor, I would like to model you like that. I cannot explain why—I am just saying what I feel. I have never felt any impulse towards art until this morning." He twisted his moustache. "Yes, you have quite an interesting face, Harden. I can see in it evidence that you have suffered intensely. You have taken life too seriously. You have worked too hard. You are stunted and deformed with work."

I regarded him with some astonishment.

"Work is all very well," he continued, "but this morning I see with singular clarity that it is only a means of development. My dear Harden, if it is overdone, it simply dwarfs the soul. Our generation has not recognized this properly."

"But you were always an apostle of hard work," I remarked irritably.

"May be." He made a gesture of dismissal. "Now, I am an Immortal, and you are an Immortal. The background to life has changed. Formerly, the idea of death lurked constantly in the depths of the unconscious mind, and by its vaguely-felt influences spurred us on to continual exertion. That is all changed. We have, at one stroke, removed this dire spectre. We are free."

He rose suddenly and flung the mirror across the room.

"What do we need mirrors for?" he cried. "It is only when we fear death that we need mirrors to tell us how long we have to live." He strode over to me and halted. "You seem in no hurry to get up from that carpet," he observed. His remark made me realize that I had been kneeling for some minutes. Now this was rather odd. I am restless by nature and rarely remain in one position for any length of time, and to stay like that, kneeling before the window, was indeed curious. I got up and moved to the dressing-table, thinking. Sarakoff must have been thinking in the same direction, for he asked me a question.

"Did you realize you were kneeling?"

"Yes," I replied. "I knew what I was doing. It merely did not occur to me that I should change my position."

59

"The explanation is simple," said the Russian. "Restlessness, or the idea that we must change our position, or that we should be doing something else, belongs to the anxious side of life; and the anxious side of life is nourished and kept vigorous by the latent fear of death. All that is removed from you, and therefore you see no reason why you should do anything until it pleases you."

I began to study myself in the glass on the dressing-table. The examination interested me immensely. There was certainly a marble-like hue about the skin. The whites of my eyes were distinctly stained, but not so intensely as had been the case with Mr. Herbert Wain, showing that I had not suffered from the Blue Disease as long as he had. But when I began to study my reflection from the æsthetic point of view, I became deeply engrossed.

"I don't agree with you, Sarakoff," I remarked at length. "We still need mirrors. In fact I have never found the mirror so interesting in my life."

"Don't use that absurd phrase," he answered. "It implies that something other than life exists."

"So it does."

"What do you mean?"

"Well, if I stick this pair of scissors into your heart you will die, my dear fellow." He was silent, and a frown began to gather on his brow. "Yes," I continued, "your psychological deductions are not entirely valid. The fear of death still exists, but now limited to a small sphere. In that sphere, it will operate with extreme intensity." I picked up the scissors and made a stealthy movement towards him. To my amazement I obtained an immediate proof of my theory. He sprang up with a loud cry, darted to the door and vanished. For a moment I stood in a state of bewilderment. Was it possible that he, with all his size and strength, was afraid of me? And then a great fit of laughter overcame me and I sank down on my bed with the tears coming from my eyes.

CHAPTER XV

THE TERRIBLE FEAR

On coming down to breakfast, I found Sarakoff already seated at the table devouring the morning papers. I picked up a discarded one and stood by the fire, glancing over its contents. There was only one subject of news, and that was the spread of the Blue Disease. From every part of the north cases were reported, and in London it had broken out in several districts.

"So it's all come true," I remarked.

He nodded, and continued reading. I sauntered to the window. A thin driving snow was now falling, and the passers-by were hurrying along in the freezing slush, with collars turned up and heads bowed before the wind.

"This is an ideal day to spend indoors by the fireside," I observed. "I think I'll telephone to the hospital and tell Jones to take my work."

Sarakoff raised his eyes, and then his eyebrows.

"So," he said, "the busy man suddenly thinks work a bother. The power of the germ, Harden, is indeed miraculous."

"Do you think my inclination is due to the germ?"

"Beyond a doubt. You were the most over-conscientious man I ever knew until this morning."

For some reason I found this observation very interesting. I wished to discuss it, and I was about to reply when the door opened and my housemaid announced that Dr. Symington-Tearle was in the hall and would like an immediate interview.

"Shew him in," I said equably. Symington-Tearle usually had a most irritating effect upon me, but at the moment I felt totally indifferent to him. He entered in his customary manner, as if the whole of London were feverishly awaiting him. I introduced Sarakoff, but Symington-Tearle hardly noticed him.

"Harden," he exclaimed in his loud dominating tones, "I am convinced that there is no such thing as this Blue Disease. I believe it all to be a colossal plant. Some practical joker has introduced a chemical into the water supply."

"Probably," I murmured, still thinking of Sarakoff's observation.

"I'm going to expose the whole thing in the evening papers; I examined a case yesterday—a man called Wain—and was convinced there was nothing wrong with him. He was really pigmented. And what is it but mere pigmentation?" He passed his hand over his brow and frowned. "Yes, yes," he continued, "that's what it is—a colossal joke. We've all been taken in by it—everyone except me." He sat down by the breakfast table suddenly and once more passed his hand over his brow.

"What was I saying?" he asked.

Sarakoff and I were now watching him intently.

"That the Blue Disease was a joke," I said.

"Ah, yes—a joke." He looked up at Sarakoff and stared for a moment. "Do you know," he said, "I believe it really is a joke."

An expression of intense solemnity came over his face, and he sat motionless gazing in front of him with unblinking eyes. I crossed to where he sat and peered at his face.

"I thought so," I remarked. "You've got it too."

"Got what?"

"The Blue Disease. I suppose you caught it from Wain, as we did." I picked up one of his hands and pointed to the faintly-tinted fingernails. Dr. Symington-Tearle stared at them with an air of such child-like simplicity and gravity that Sarakoff and I broke into loud laughter.

The humour of the situation passed with a peculiar suddenness and we ceased laughing abruptly. I sat down at the table, and for some time the three of us gazed at one another and said nothing. The spirit-lamp that heated the silver dish of bacon upon the table spurted at intervals and I saw Symington-Tearle stare at it in faint surprise.

"Does it sound very loud?" asked Sarakoff at length.

"Extraordinarily loud. And upon my soul your voice nearly deafens me."

"It will pass," I said. "One gets adjusted to the extreme sensitiveness in a short time. How do you feel?"

"I feel," said Symington-Tearle slowly, "as if I were newly constructed from the crown of my head to the soles of my feet. After a Turkish bath and twenty minutes' massage I've experienced a little of the feeling."

He stared at Sarakoff, then at me, and finally at the spirit lamp. We must have presented an odd spectacle. For there we sat, three men who, under ordinary circumstances, were extremely busy and active, lolling round the unfinished breakfast table while the hands of the clock travelled relentlessly onward.

Relentlessly? That was scarcely correct. To me, owing to some mysterious change that I cannot explain, the clock had ceased to be a tyrannous and hateful monster. I did not care how fast it went or to what hour it pointed. Time was no longer precious, any more than the sand of the sea is precious.

"Aren't you going to have any breakfast?" asked Symington-Tearle.

"I'm not in the least hurry," replied Sarakoff. "I think I'll take a sip of coffee. Are you hungry, Harden?"

"No. I don't want anything save coffee. But I'm in no hurry."

My housemaid entered and announced that the gentleman who had been waiting in Dr. Symington-Tearle's car, and was now in the hall, wished to know if the doctor would be long.

"Oh, that is a patient of mine," said Symington-Tearle, "ask him to come in."

A large, stout, red-faced gentleman entered, wrapped in a thick frieze motor coat. He nodded to us briefly.

"Sorry to interrupt," he said, "but time's getting on, Tearle. My consultation with Sir Peverly Salt was for half past nine, if you remember. It's that now."

"Oh, there's plenty of time," said Tearle. "Sit down, Ballard. It's nice and warm in here."

"It may be nice and warm," replied Mr. Ballard loudly, "but I don't want to keep Sir Peverly waiting."

"I don't see why you shouldn't keep him waiting," said Tearle. "In fact I really don't see why you should go to him at all."

Mr. Ballard stared for a moment. Then his eyes travelled round the table and dwelt first on Sarakoff and then on me. I suppose something in our manner rather baffled him, but outwardly he shewed no sign of it.

"I don't quite follow you," he said, fixing his gaze upon Tearle again. "If you recollect, you advised me strongly four days ago to consult Sir Peverly Salt about the condition of my heart, and you impressed upon me that his opinion was the best that was obtainable. You rang him up and an appointment was fixed for this morning at half-past nine, and I was told to call on you shortly after nine."

He paused, and once more his eyes dwelt in turn upon each of us. They returned to Tearle. "It is now twenty-five minutes to ten," he said. His face had become redder, and his voice louder. "And I understood that Sir Peverly is a very busy man."

"He certainly is busy," said Tearle. "He's far too busy. It is very interesting to think that business is only necessary in so far——"

63

"Look here," said Mr. Ballard violently. "I'm a man with a short temper. I'm hanged if I'll stand this nonsense. What the devil do you think you're all doing? Are you playing a joke on me?"

He glared round at us, and then he made a sudden movement towards the table. In a moment we were all on our feet. I felt an acute terror seize me, and without waiting to see what happened, I flung open the door that led into my consulting room, darted to the further door, across the hall and up to my bedroom.

There was a cry and a rush of feet across the hall. Mr. Ballard's voice rang out stormily. A door slammed, and then another door, and then all was silent.

I became aware of a movement behind me, and looking round sharply, I saw my housemaid Lottie staring at me in amazement. She had been engaged in making the bed.

"Whatever is the matter, sir?" she asked.

"Hush!" I whispered. "There's a dangerous man downstairs."

I turned the key in the lock, listened for a moment, and then tip-toed my way across the floor to a chair. My limbs were shaking. It is difficult to describe the intensity of my terror. There was a cold sweat on my forehead. "He might have killed me. Think of that!"

Her eyes were fixed on me.

"Oh, sir, you do look bad," she exclaimed. "Whatever has happened to you?" She came nearer and gazed into my eyes. "They're all blue, sir. It must be that disease you've got."

A sudden irritation flashed over me. "Don't stare at me like that. You'll have it yourself to-morrow," I shouted. "The whole of the blessed city will have it." A loud rap at the door interrupted me. I jumped up, darted across the room and threw myself under the bed. "Don't let anyone in," I whispered. The rap was repeated. Sarakoff's voice sounded without.

"Let me in. It's all right. He's gone. The front door is bolted." I crawled out and unlocked the door. Sarakoff, looking rather pale, was standing in the passage. He carried a poker. "Symington-Tearle's in the coal-cellar," he announced. "He won't come out."

I wiped my brow with a handkerchief.

"Good heavens, Sarakoff," I exclaimed, "this kind of thing will lead to endless trouble. I had no idea the terror would be so uncontrollable."

"I'm glad you feel it as I do," said the Russian. "When you threatened me with a pair of scissors this morning I felt mad with fear."

"It's awful," I murmured. "We can't be too careful." We began to descend the stairs. "Sarakoff, you remember I told you about that

64

dead sailor? I see now why that expression was on his face. It was the terror that he felt."

"Extraordinary!" he muttered. "He couldn't have known. It must have been instinctive."

"Instincts are like that," I said. "I don't suppose an animal knows anything about death, or even thinks of it, yet it behaves from the very first as if it knew. It's odd."

A door opened at the far end of the hall, and Symington-Tearle emerged. There was a patch of coal-dust on his forehead. His hair, usually so flat and smooth that it seemed like a brass mirror, was now disordered.

"Has he gone?" he enquired hoarsely.

We nodded. I pointed to the chain on the door.

"It's bolted," I said. "Come into the study."

I led the way into the room. Tearle walked to the window, then to a chair, and finally took up a position before the fire.

"This is extraordinary!" he exclaimed.

"What do you make of it?" I asked.

"I can make nothing of it. What's the matter with me? I never felt anything like that terror that came over me when Ballard approached me."

Sarakoff took out a large handkerchief and passed it across his face. "It's only the fear of physical violence," he said. "That's the only weak spot. Fear was formerly distributed over a wide variety of possibilities, but now it's all concentrated in one direction."

"Why?" Tearle stared at me questioningly.

"Because the germ is in us," I said. "We're immortal."

"Immortal?"

Sarakoff threw out his hands, and flung back his head. "Immortals!"

I crossed to my writing-table, and picked up a heavy volume.

"Here is the first edition of Buckwell Pink's System of Medicine. This book was produced at immense cost and labour, and it is to be published next week. When that book is published no one will buy it."

"Why not?" demanded Tearle. "I wrote an article in it myself."

"So did I," was my reply. "But that won't make any difference. No member of the medical profession will be interested in it."

"Not interested? I can't believe that. It contains all the recent work."

"The medical profession will not be interested in it for a very simple reason. The medical profession will have ceased to exist."

A look of amazement came to Tearle's face. I tapped the volume and continued.

"You are wrong in thinking it contains all the recent work. It does not. The last and greatest achievement of medical science is not recorded in these pages. It is only recorded in ourselves. For that blue pigmentation in your eyes and fingers is due to the Sarakoff-Harden bacillus which closes once and for all the chapter of medicine."

CHAPTER XVI

THE VISIT OF THE HOME SECRETARY

In a few hours the initial effects of stimulation had worn off. The acuity of hearing was no longer so pronounced and the sense of refreshment, although still present, was not intense. We were already becoming adjusted to the new condition. The feeling of inertia and irresponsibility became gradually replaced by a general sense of calmness. To me, it seemed as if I had entered a world of new perspectives, a larger world in which space and time were widened out immeasurably. I could scarcely recall the nature of those impulses that had once driven me to and fro in endless activities, and in a constant state of anxiety. For now I had no anxiety.

It is difficult to describe fully the extraordinary sense of freedom that came from this change. For anxiety—the great modern emotion—is something that besets a life on all sides so silently and so continuously that it escapes direct detection. But it is there, tightening the muscles, crinkling the skin, quickening the heart and shortening the breath. Though almost imperceptible, it lurks under the most agreeable surroundings, requiring only a word or a look to bring it into the light. To be free from it—ah, that was an experience that no man could ever forget! It was perhaps the nearest approach to that condition of bliss, which many expect in one of the Heavens, that had ever been attained on earth. As long as no physical danger threatened, this bliss-state surrounded me. Its opposite, that condition of violent, agonizing, uncontrollable fear that suddenly surged over one on the approach of bodily danger, was something which passed as swiftly as it came, and left scarcely a trace behind it. But of that I shall have more to say, for it produced the most extraordinary state of affairs and more than anything else threatened to disorganize life completely.

I fancy Sarakoff was more awed by the bliss-state than I was. During the rest of the day he was very quiet and sat gazing before him His boisterousness had vanished. Symington-Tearle had left us—a man deeply amazed and totally incredulous. I noticed that Sarakoff scarcely smoked at all during that morning. As a rule his pipe was never out. He was in the habit of consuming two ounces of tobacco a day, which in my opinion was suicidal. He certainly lit his pipe several times, mechanically, but laid it aside almost immediately. At lunch—we had not moved out of the house yet—we had very little appetite. As a matter of interest I will give exactly what we ate and drank. Sarakoff took some soup and a piece of bread, and then some cheese. I began with some cold beef, and finding it unattractive, pushed it away and ate some biscuits and butter. There was claret on the table. I wish here to call attention to a passing impression that I experienced when sipping that claret. I had recently got in several dozen bottles of it and on that day regretted it because it seemed to me to be extremely poor stuff. It tasted sour and harsh.

We did not talk much. It was not because my mind was devoid of ideas, but rather because I was feeling that I had a prodigious, incalculable amount to think about. Perhaps it was the freedom from anxiety that made thinking easier, for there is little doubt that anxiety, however masked, deflects and disturbs the power of thought more than anything else. Indeed it seemed to me that I had never really thought clearly before. To begin a conversation with Sarakoff seemed utterly artificial. It would have been a useless interruption. I was entirely absorbed.

Sarakoff was similarly absorbed. When, therefore, the servant came in to announce that two gentlemen wished to see us, and were in the waiting-room, we were loth to move. I got up at length and went across the hall. I recollect that before entering the waiting-room I was entirely without curiosity. It was a matter of total indifference to me that two visitors were within. They had no business to interrupt me—that was my feeling. They were intruders and should have known better.

I entered the room. Standing by the fire was Lord Alberan. Beside him was a tall thin man, carefully dressed and something of a dandy, who looked at me sharply as I came across the room. I recognized his face, but failed to recall his name.

Lord Alberan, holding himself very stiffly, cleared his throat.

"Good day, Dr. Harden," he said, without offering his hand. "I have brought Sir Robert Smith to interview you. As you may know he is the Home Secretary." He cleared his throat again, and his face became rather red. "I have reported to the Home Secretary the information that I—er—that I acquired from you and your Russian companion concerning this epidemic that has swept over Birmingham and is now threatening London." He paused and stared at me. His eyes bulged. "Good heavens," he exclaimed, "you've got it yourself."

Sir Robert Smith took a step towards me and examined my face attentively.

"Yes," he said, "there's no doubt you've got it."

I indicated some chairs with a calm gesture.

"Won't you sit down?"

Lord Alberan refused, but Sir Robert lowered himself gracefully into an arm-chair and crossed his legs.

"Dr. Harden," he said, in smooth and pleasant tones, "I wish you to understand that I come here, at this unusual hour, solely in the spirit of one who desires to get all the information possible concerning the malady, called the Blue Disease, which is now sweeping over England. I understand from my friend Lord Alberan, that you know something about it."

"That is true."

"How much do you know?"

"I know all there is to be known."

"Ah!" Sir Robert leaned forward. Lord Alberan nodded violently and glared at me. There was a pause. "What you say is very interesting," said Sir Robert at length, keeping his eyes fixed upon me. "You understand, of course, that the Blue Disease is causing a lot of anxiety?"

"Anxiety?" I exclaimed. "Surely you are wrong. It has the opposite effect. It abolishes anxiety."

"You mean——?" he queried politely.

"I mean that the germ, when once in the system, produces an atmosphere of extraordinary calm," I returned. "I am aware of that atmosphere at this moment. I have never felt so perfectly tranquil before."

He nodded, without moving his eyes.

"So I see. You struck me, as you came into the room, as a man who is at peace with himself." Lord Alberan snorted, and was about to speak, but Sir Robert held up his hand. "Tell me, Dr. Harden, did you actually contaminate the water of Birmingham?"

"My friend Sarakoff and I introduced the germ that we discovered into the Elan reservoirs."

"With what object?"

"To endow humanity with the gift of immortality."

"Ah!" he nodded gently. "The gift of immortality." He mused for a moment, and never once did his eyes leave my face. "That is interesting," he continued. "I recollect that at the International Congress at Moscow, a few years ago, there was much talk about longevity. Virchow, I fancy, and Nikola Tesla made some suggestive remarks. So you think you have discovered the secret?"

"I am sure."

"Of course you use the term immortality in a relative sense?

69

You mean that the—er—germ that you discovered confers a long life on those it attacks?"

"I mean what I say. It confers immortality."

"Indeed!" His expression remained perfectly polite and interested, but his eyes turned for a brief moment in the direction of Lord Alberan. "So you are now immortal, Dr. Harden?"

"Yes."

"And will you, in such circumstances, go on practising medicine—indefinitely?"

"No. There will be no medicine to practise."

"Ah!" he nodded. "I see—the germ does away with disease. Quite so." He leaned back in the chair and pressed his finger tips together. "I suppose," he continued, "that you are aware that what you say is very difficult to believe?"

"Why?"

"Well, the artificial prolongation of life is, I believe, a possibility that we are all prepared to accept. By special methods we may live a few extra years, and everything goes to show that we are actually living longer than our ancestors. At least I believe so. But for a man of your position, Dr. Harden, to say that the epidemic is an epidemic of immortality is, in my opinion, an extravagant statement."

"You are entitled to any opinion you like," I replied tranquilly. "It is possible to live with totally erroneous opinions. For all I know you may think the earth is square. It makes no difference to me."

"What do you mean, sir?" exclaimed Lord Alberan. He had become exceedingly red during our conversation and the lower part of his face had begun to swell. "Be careful what you say," he continued violently. "You are in danger of being arrested, sir. Either that, or being locked in an asylum."

The Home Secretary raised a restraining hand.

"One moment, Lord Alberan," he said, "I have not quite finished. Dr. Harden, will you be so good as to ask your friend—his name is Sarakoff, I believe—to come in here?"

I rose without haste and fetched the Russian. He behaved in an extremely quiet manner, nodded to Alberan and bowed to the Home Secretary.

Sir Robert gave a brief outline of the conversation he had had with me, which Sarakoff listened to with an absolutely expressionless face.

"I see that you also suffer from the epidemic," said Sir Robert. "Are you, then, immortal?"

"I am an Immortal," said the Russian, in deep tones. "You will be immortal to-morrow."

70

"I quite understand that I will probably catch the Blue Disease," said Sir Robert, suavely. "At present there are cases reported all over London, and we are at a loss to know what to do."

"You can do nothing," I said.

"We had thought of forming isolation camps." He stared at us thoughtfully. There was a slightly puzzled look in his face. It was the first time I had noticed it. It must have been due to Sarakoff's profound calm. "How did you gentlemen find the germ?" he asked suddenly.

Sarakoff reflected.

"It would take perhaps a week to explain."

Sir Robert smiled slightly.

"I'm afraid I am too busy," he murmured.

"You are wasting your time," muttered Alberan in his ear. "Arrest them."

The Home Secretary took no notice.

"It is curious that this epidemic seems to cut short other diseases," he said slowly. "That rather supports what you tell me."

His eyes rested searchingly on my face.

"You are foolish to refuse to believe us," I said. "We have told you the truth."

"It would be very strange if it were true." He walked to the window and stood for a moment looking on to the street. Then he turned with a movement of resolution. "I will not trespass on your time," he said. "Lord Alberan, we need not stay. I am satisfied with what these gentlemen have said." He bowed to us and went to the door. Lord Alberan, very fierce and upright, followed him. The Home Secretary paused and looked back. The puzzled looked had returned to his face.

"The matter is to be discussed in the House to-night," he said. "I think that it will be as well for you if I say nothing of what you have told me. People might be angry." We gazed at him unmoved. He took a sudden step towards us and held out his hands. "Come now, gentlemen, tell me the truth. You invented that story, didn't you?" Neither of us spoke. He looked appealingly at me, and with a laugh left the room. He turned, however, in a moment, and stood looking at me. "There is a meeting at the Queen's Hall to-night," he said slowly. "It is a medical conference on the Blue Disease. No doubt you know of it. I am going to ask you a question." He paused and smiled at Sarakoff. "Will you gentlemen make a statement before those doctors to-night?"

"We intended to do so," said Sarakoff.

"I am delighted to hear it," said the Home Secretary. "It is a great relief to me. They will know how best to deal with you. Good day."

He left the room.

I heard the front door close and then brisk footsteps passing the window on the pavement outside.

"There's no doubt that they're both a little mad." Sir Robert's voice sounded for a moment, and then died away.

CHAPTER XVII

CLUTTERBUCK'S ODD BEHAVIOUR

Scarcely had the Home Secretary departed when my maid announced that a patient was waiting to see me in my study.

I left Sarakoff sitting tranquilly in the waiting-room and entered the study. A grave, precise, clean-shaven man was standing by the window. He turned as I entered. It was Mr. Clutterbuck.

"So you are Dr. Harden!" he exclaimed.

He stopped and looked confused.

"Yes," I said; "please sit down, Mr. Clutterbuck."

He did so, twisting his hat awkwardly and gazing at the floor.

"I owe you an apology," he said at length. "I came to consult you, little expecting to find that it was you after all—that you were Dr. Harden. I must apologize for my rudeness to you in the tea-shop, but what you said was so extraordinary ... you could not expect me to believe."

He glanced at me, and then looked away. There was a dull flush on his face.

"Please do not apologize. What did you wish to consult me about?"

"About my wife."

"Is she worse?"

"No." He dropped his hat, recovered it, and finally set it upon a corner of the table. "No, she is not worse. In fact, she is the reverse. She is better."

I waited, feeling only a mild interest in the cause of his agitation.

"She has got the Blue Disease," he continued, speaking with difficulty. "She got it yesterday and since then she has been much better. Her cough has ceased. She—er—she is wonderfully better." He began to drum with his fingers on his knee, and looked with a vacant gaze at the corner of the room. "Yes, she is certainly better. I was wondering if——"

There was a silence.

"Yes?"

He started and looked at me.

"Why, you've got it, too!" he exclaimed. "How extraordinary! I

73

hadn't noticed it." He got to his feet and went to the window. "I suppose I shall get it next," he muttered.

"Certainly, you'll get it."

He nodded, and continued to stare out of the window. At length he spoke.

"My wife is a woman who has suffered a great deal, Dr. Harden. I have never had enough money to send her to health resorts, and she has always refused to avail herself of any institutional help. For the last year she has been confined to a room on the top floor of our house—a nice, pleasant room—and it has been an understood thing between Dr. Sykes and myself that her malady was to be given a convenient name. In fact, we have called it a weak heart. You understand, of course."

"Perfectly."

"I have always been led to expect that the end was inevitable," he continued, speaking with sudden rapidity. "Under such circumstances I made certain plans. I am a careful man, Dr. Harden, and I look ahead and lay my plans." He stopped abruptly and turned to face me. "Is there any truth in what you told me the other day?"

I nodded. A curiously haggard expression came over him. He stepped swiftly towards me and caught my arm.

"Does the germ cure disease?"

"Of course. Your wife is now immortal. You need not be alarmed, Mr. Clutterbuck. She is immortal. Before her lies a future absolutely free from suffering. She will rapidly regain her normal health and strength. Provided she avoids accidents, your wife will live for ever."

"My wife will live forever?" he repeated hoarsely. "Then what will happen to me?"

"You, too, will live for ever," I said calmly. "Please do not grasp my arm so violently."

He drew back. He was extremely pale, and there were beads of perspiration on his brow.

"Are you married?" he asked.

"No."

"Have you any idea what all this means to me if what you say is true?" he exclaimed. He drew his hand across his eyes. "I am mad to believe you for an instant. But she is better—there is no denying that. Good God, if it is true, what a tragedy you have made of human lives!"

He remained standing in the middle of the room, and I, not

comprehending, gazed at him. Then, of a sudden, he picked up his hat, and muttering something, dashed out and vanished.

I heard the front door bang. Perfectly calm and undisturbed, I rejoined Sarakoff in the waiting-room. The incident of Mr. Clutterbuck passed totally from my mind, and I began to reflect on certain problems arising out of the visit of the Home Secretary.

CHAPTER XVIII

IMMORTAL LOVE

On the same afternoon Miss Annot paid me a visit. I was still sitting in the waiting-room, and Sarakoff was with me. My mind had been deeply occupied with the question of the larger beliefs that we hold. For it had come to me with peculiar force that law and order, and officials like the Home Secretary, are concerned only with the small beliefs of humanity, with the burdensome business of material life. As long as a man dressed properly, walked decently and paid correctly, he was accepted, in spite of the fact that he might firmly believe the world was square. No one worried about those matters. We judge people ultimately by how they eat and drink and get up and sit down. What they say is of little importance in the long run. If we examine a person professionally, we merely ask him what day it is, where he is, what is his name and where he was born. We watch him to see if he washes, undresses and dresses, and eats properly. We ask him to add two and two, and to divide six by three, and then we solemnly give our verdict that he is either sane or insane.

The enormity of this revelation engrossed me with an almost painful activity of thought.

I gazed across at Sarakoff and wondered what appalling gulf divided our views on supreme things. What view did he really take of women? Did he or did he not think that the planets and stars were inhabited? Did he believe in the evolution of the soul like Mr. Thornduck?

A kind of horror possessed me as I stared at him and reflected that these questions had never entered my consciousness until that moment. I had lived with him and dined with him and worked with him, and yet hitherto it would have concerned me far more if I had seen him tuck his napkin under his collar or spit on the carpet.... What laughable little folk we were! I, who had always seen man as the last and final expression of evolution, now saw him as the stumbling, crawling, incredibly stupid, result of a tentative experiment—a first step up a ladder of infinitive length.

Whilst I was immersed in the humiliation of these thoughts Miss Annot entered. She wore a dark violet coat and skirt and a black hat. I noticed that her complexion, usually somewhat muddy, was perfectly clear, though of a marble pallor. We greeted each other quietly and I introduced Sarakoff.

"So you are an Immortal, Alice," I said smiling. She gazed at me.

"Richard, I do not know what I am, but I know one thing; I am entirely changed. Some strange miracle has been wrought in me. I came to ask you what it is."

"You see that both Professor Sarakoff and I have got the germ in our systems like you, Alice. Yes, it is a miracle; we are Immortals."

I studied her face attentively, she had changed. It seemed to me that she was another woman, she moved in a new way, her speech was unhurried, her gaze was direct and thoughtful. I recalled her former appearance when her manner had been nervous and bashful, her eyes downcast, her movements hurried and anxious.

"I do not understand," she said. "Tell me all you know."

I did so, I suppose I must have talked for an hour on end. Throughout that time neither she nor Sarakoff stirred. When I had finished there was a long silence.

"It is funny to think of our last meeting, Richard," she said at length. "Do you remember how my father behaved? He is different now. He sits all day in his study—he eats very little. He seems to be in a dream."

"And you?" I asked.

"I am in a dream, too. I do not understand it. All the things I used to busy myself with seem unimportant."

"That is how we feel," said Sarakoff. He rose to his feet and spoke strongly. "Harden, as Miss Annot says, everything has changed. I never foresaw this; I do not understand it myself."

He went slowly to the mantelpiece and leaned against it.

"When I created this germ, I saw in my mind an ideal picture of life. I saw a world freed from a dire spectre, a world from which fear had been removed, the fear of death. I saw the great triumph of materialism and the final smashing up of all superstition. A man would live in a state of absolute certainty. He would lay his plans for pleasure and comfort and enjoyment with absolute precision, knowing—not hoping—but certainly knowing, that they would come about. I saw cities and gardens built in triumph to cater for the gratification of every sense. I saw new laws in operation, constructed by men who knew that they had mastered the secret of life and had nothing to fear. I saw all those things about which we are so timid and vague—marriage and divorce, the education of children, luxury, the working classes, religion and so on—absolutely

77

settled in black and white. I saw what I thought to be the millennium."

"And now?" asked Alice.

"Now I see nothing. I am in the dark. I do not understand what has happened to me."

"What we are in for now, no man can say," I remarked.

"It's the extraordinary restfulness that puzzles me," said Sarakoff. "Here I have been sitting for hours and I feel no inclination to do anything."

"The thing that is most extraordinary to me is the difficulty I have in realizing how I spent my time formerly," said Alice. "Of course, father is no bother now and meals have been cut down, but that does not account for all of it. It seems as if I had been living in a kind of nightmare in the past, from which I have suddenly escaped."

"What do you feel most inclined to do?" I asked.

"Nothing at present. I sit and think. It was difficult for me to make myself come here to-day." She smiled suddenly. "Richard, it seems strange to recall that we were engaged."

She spoke without any embarrassment and I answered her with equal ease.

"I hope you don't think our engagement is broken off, Alice. I think my feelings towards you are unchanged."

"Ah!" exclaimed Sarakoff. "That is interesting. Are you sure of that, Harden?"

"Not altogether," I answered tranquilly. "There is a lot to think out before I can be sure, but I know that I feel towards Alice a great sympathy."

"Sympathy!" the Russian exclaimed. "What are we coming to? Good heavens! Is sympathy to be our strongest emotion? What do you think, Miss Annot."

"Sympathy is exactly what I feel," she replied. "Richard and I would be very good companions. Isn't that more important than passion?"

"Is sympathy to be the bond between the sexes, then, and is all passion and romance to die?" he exclaimed scornfully. He seemed to be struggling with himself, as if he were trying to throw off some spell that held him. "Surely I seem to recollect that yesterday life contained some richer emotions than sympathy," he muttered. "What has come over us? Why doesn't my blood quicken when I think of Leonora?" He burst into a laugh. "Harden, this is comic. There is no other word for it. It is simply comic."

"It may be comic, Sarakoff, but to speak candidly, I prefer my state to-day to my state yesterday. Last night seems to me like a bad dream." I got to my feet. "There is one thing I must see about as soon as possible, and that is getting rid of this house. What an absurd place to live in this is! It is a comic house, if you like—like a tomb."

The room seemed suddenly absurd. It was very dark, the wallpaper was of a heavy-moulded variety, sombre in hue and covered with meaningless figuring. The ceiling was oppressive. It, too, was moulded in some fantastic manner. Several large faded oil-paintings hung on the wall. I do not know why they hung there, they were hideous and meaningless as well. The whole place was meaningless. It was the meaninglessness that seemed to leap out upon me wherever I turned my eyes. The fireplace astounded me. It was a mass of pillars and super-structures and carvings, increasing in complexity from within outwards, until it attained the appearance of an ornate temple in the centre of which burned a little coal. It was grotesque. On the topmost ledges of this monstrous absurdity stood two vases. They bulged like distended stomachs, covered on their outsides with yellow, green and black splotches of colour. I recollected that I paid ten pounds apiece for them. Under what perverted impulse had I done that? My memories became incredible. I moved deliberately to the mantelpiece and seized the vases. I opened the window and hurled them out on to the pavement. They fell with a crash, and their fragments littered the ground.

Alice expressed no surprise.

"It is rather comic," said the Russian, "but where are you going to live?"

"Alice and I will go and live by the sea. We have plenty to think about. I feel as if I could never stop thinking, as if I had to dig away a mountain of thought with a spade. Alice, we will go round to the house agent now."

When Alice and I left the house the remains of the vases littered the pavement at our feet. We walked down Harley Street. The house agent lived in Regent Street. It was now a clear, crisp afternoon with a pleasant tint of sunlight in the air. A newspaper boy passed, calling something unintelligible in an excited voice. I stopped him and bought a paper.

"What an inhuman noise to make," said Alice. "It seems to jar on every nerve in my body. Do ask him to stop."

"You're making too much noise," I said tothe lad. "You must call softly. It is an outrage to scream like that."

He stared up at me, an impudent amazed face surmounting a tattered and dishevelled body, and spoke.

"You two do look a couple of guys, wiv' yer blue faices. If some of them doctors round 'ere catches yer, they'll pop yer into 'ospital."

He ran off, shrieking his unintelligible jargon.

"We must get to the sea," I said firmly. "This clamour of London is unbearable."

I opened the paper. Enormous headlines stared me in the face.

"Blue Disease sweeping over London. Ten thousand cases reported to-day. Europe alarmed. Question of the isolation of Great Britain under discussion. Debate in the Commons to-night. The Duke of Thud and the Earl of Blunder victims. The Royal Family leave London."

We stood together on the pavement and gazed at these statements in silence. A sense of wonder filled my mind. What a confusion! What an emotional, feverish, heated confusion! Why could not they take the matter calmly? What, in the name of goodness, was the reason of this panic. They knew that the Blue Disease had caused no fatalities in Birmingham, and yet so totally absent was the power of thought and deduction, that they actually printed those glaring headlines.

"The fools," I said. "The amazing, fatuous fools. They simply want to sell the paper. They have no other idea."

A strong nausea came over me. I crumpled up the paper and stood staring up and down the street. The newspaper boy was in the far distance, still shrieking. I saw Sir Barnaby Burtle, the obstetrician, standing by his scarlet front door, eagerly devouring the news. His jaw was slack and his eyes protruded.

The solemn houses of Harley Street only increased my nausea. The folly of it—the selfish, savage folly of life!

"Come, Richard," said Alice. "The sooner we get to the house agent the better. We could never live here."

"I'll put him on to the job of finding a bungalow on the South Coast at once," I said. "And then we'll go and live there."

"We must get married," she observed.

"Married!" I stopped and stared at her with a puzzled expression. "Don't you think the marriage ceremony is rather barbarous?"

She did not reply; we walked on immersed in our own thoughts. At times I detected in the passers-by a gleam of sparrow-egg blue.

My house agent was a large, confused individual who habitually wore a shining top hat on the back of his head and twisted a cigar in the corner of his mouth. He was very fat, with one of those creased faces that seem to fall into folds like a heavy crimson curtain. His brooding, congested eye fell upon me as we entered, and an expression of alarm became visible in its depths. He pushed his chair back and retreated to a corner of the room.

"Dr. Harden!" he exclaimed fearfully, "you oughtn't to come here like that, you really oughtn't."

"Don't be an ass, Franklyn," I said firmly. "You are bound to catch the germ sooner or later. It will impress you immensely."

"It's all over London," he whimpered. "It's too much; it will hit us hard. It's too much."

"Listen to me," I said. "I have come here to see you about business. Now sit down in your chair; I won't touch you. I want you to get me a bungalow by the sea with a garden as soon as possible. I am going to sell my house."

"Sell your house!" He became calmer. "That is very extraordinary, Dr. Harden."

"I am going out of London."

He was astonished.

"But your house—in Harley Street—so central...." he stammered. "I don't understand. Are you giving up your practice?"

"Of course."

"At your age, Dr. Harden?"

"What has age got to do with it? There is no such thing as age."

He stared. Then his eyes turned to Alice.

"No such thing as age?" he murmured helplessly. "But surely you are not going to sell; you have the best house in Harley Street. Its commanding position ... in the centre of that famous locality...."

"Do you think that any really sane man would live in the centre of Harley Street," I asked calmly. "Is he likely to find any peace in that furnace of crude worldly ambitions? But all that is already a thing of the past. In a few weeks, Franklyn, Harley Street will be deserted."

"Deserted?" His eyes rolled.

"Deserted," I said sternly. "In its upper rooms there may remain a few Immortals, but the streets will be silent. The great business of sickness, which occupies the attention of a third of the world and furnishes the main topic of conversation in every home, will be gone. Sell my house, Franklyn, and find me a bungalow on the South Coast facing the sea."

I turned away and went towards the door, Alice followed me. The house agent sat in helpless amazement. He filled me with a sense of nausea. He seemed so gross, so mindless.

"A bungalow," he whispered.

"Yes. Let us have long, low, simple rooms and a garden where we may grow enough to live on. The age of material complexity and noise is at an end. We need peace."

Strolling along at a slow pace, we went down Oxford Street towards the Marble Arch. It was dusk. The newsboys were howling at every corner and everyone had a paper. Little groups of people stood on the pavements discussing the news. In the roadway the stream of traffic was incessant. The huge motor-buses thundered and swayed along, with their loads of pale humanity feverishly clinging to them. The public-houses were crowded. The slight tension that the threat of the Blue Disease produced in people filled the bars with men and women, seeking the relaxation of alcohol. There was in the air that liveliness, that tendency to collect into small crowds, that is evident whenever the common safety of the great herd is threatened. In the Park a crowd surrounded the platform of an agitator. In a voice like that of a delirious man, he implored the crowd to go down on its knees and repent ... the end of the world was at hand ... the Blue Disease was the pouring out of one of the vials of wrath ... repent!... repent!... His voice rang in our ears and drove us away. We crossed the damp grass. I stumbled over a sleeping man. There was something familiar in his appearance and I stooped down and turned him over. It was Mr. Herbert Wain. He seemed to be fast asleep.... We walked to King's Cross, and I put Alice without regret in the train for Cambridge.

CHAPTER XIX

THE MEETING AT THE QUEEN'S HALL

The same night a vast meeting of medical men had been summoned at the Queen's Hall, with the object of discussing the nature of the strange visitation, and the measures that should be adopted. Doctors came from every part of the country. The meeting began at eight o'clock, and Sir Jeremy Jones, the President of the Royal College of Physicians, opened the discussion with a paper in which the most obvious features of the disease were briefly tabulated.

The great Hall was packed. Sarakoff and I got seats in the front row of the gallery. Sir Jeremy Jones, a large bland man, with beautiful silver grey hair, wearing evening dress, and pince-nez, stood up on the platform amid a buzz of talk. The short outburst of clapping soon ceased and Sir Jeremy began.

The beginnings of the disease were outlined, the symptoms described, and then the physician laid down his notes, and seemed to look directly up at me.

"So far," he said, in suave and measured tones, "I have escaped the Blue Disease, but at any moment I may find myself a victim, and the fact does not disquiet me. For I am convinced that we are witnessing the sudden intrusion and the swift spread of an absolutely harmless organism—one that has been, perhaps, dormant for centuries in the soil, or has evolved to its present form in the deep waters of the Elan watershed by a process whose nature we can only dimly guess at. Some have suggested a meteoric origin, and it is true that some meteoric stones fell over Wales recently. But that is far-fetched to my mind, for how could a white-hot stone harbour living matter? Whatever its origin, it is, I am sure, a harmless thing, and though strange, and at first sight alarming, we need none of us alter our views of life or our way of living. The subject is now open for discussion, and I call on Professor Sarakoff, of Petrograd, the eminent bacteriologist, to give us the benefit of his views, as I believe he has a statement to make."

A burst of applause filled the Hall.

"Good," muttered Sarakoff in my ear. "I will certainly give them my views."

"Be careful," I said idly. Sir Jeremy was gazing round the Hall.

Sarakoff stood up and there arose cries for silence. He made a striking figure with his giant stature, his black hair and beard and his blue-stained eyes. Sir Jeremy sat down, smiling blandly.

"Mr. President and Gentlemen," began the Professor, in a voice that carried to every part of the Hall. "I, as an Immortal, desire to make a few simple and decisive statements to you to-night regarding the nature of the Blue Disease, the germ of which was prepared by myself and my friend, Dr. Richard Harden. The germ—in future to be known as the Sarakoff-Harden bacillus—is ultra-microscopical. It grows in practically every medium with great ease. In the human body it finds an admirable host, and owing to the fact that it destroys all other organisms, it confers immortality on the person who is infected by it. We are therefore on the threshold of a new era."

After this brief statement Sarakoff calmly sat down, and absolute silence reigned. Sir Jeremy, still smiling blandly, stared up at him. Every face was turned in our direction. A murmur began, which quickly increased. A doctor behind me leaned over and touched my shoulder.

"Is he sane?" he asked in a whisper.

"Perfectly," I replied.

"But you don't believe him?"

"Of course I do."

"But it's ridiculous! Who is this Dr. Harden?"

"I am Dr. Harden."

The uproar in the Hall was now considerable. Sir Jeremy rose, and waved his hands in gestures of restraint. Finally he had recourse to a bell that stood on the table.

"Gentlemen," he said, when silence was restored. "We have just heard a remarkable statement from Professor Sarakoff and I think I am justified in asking for proofs."

I instantly got up. I was quite calm.

"I can prove that Sarakoff's statement is perfectly correct," I said. "I am Richard Harden. I discovered the method whereby the bacillus became a possibility. Every man in this Hall who has the Sarakoff-Harden bacillus in his system is immortal. You, Mr. President, are not yet one of the Immortals. But I fancy in a day or two you will join us." I paused and smiled easily at the concourse below and around me. "It is really bad luck on the medical profession," I continued. "I'm afraid we'll all have to find some other occupation. Of course you've all noticed how the germ cuts short disease."

84

I sat down again. The smile on Sir Jeremy's face had weakened a little.

"Turn them out!" shouted an angry voice from the body of the Hall.

Sir Jeremy held up a protesting hand, and then took off his glasses and began to polish them. A buzz of talk arose. Men turned to one another and began to argue. The doctor behind me leaned forward again.

"Is this a joke?" he enquired rather loudly.

"No."

"But you two are speaking rubbish. What the devil do you mean by saying you're immortal?"

I turned and looked at him. My calmness enraged him. He was a shaggy, irritable, middle-aged practitioner.

"You've got the Blue Disease, but you're no more immortal than a blue monkey." He looked fiercely round at his neighbours. "What do you think?"

A babel of voices sounded in our ears.

Sir Jeremy Jones appeared perplexed. Someone stood up in the body of the Hall and Sir Jeremy caught his eye and seemed relieved. It was my friend Hammer, who had tended me after the accident that my black cat had brought about.

"Gentlemen," said Hammer, when silence had fallen. "Although the statements of Professor Sarakoff and Dr. Harden appear fantastical, I believe that they may be nearer the truth than we suppose." His manner, slow, impressive and calm, aroused general attention. Frowning slightly, he drew himself up and clasped the lapels of his coat. "This afternoon," he continued, "I was at the bedside of a sick child who was at the point of death. This child had been visited yesterday by a relative who, two hours after the visit, developed the Blue Disease. Now——" He paused and looked slowly about him. "Now the child was suffering from peritonitis, and there was no possible chance of recovery. Yet that child did recover and is now well."

The whole audience was staring at him. Hammer took a deep breath and grasped his coat more firmly.

"That child, I repeat, is now well. The recovery set in under my own eyes. I saw for myself the return of life to a body that was moribund. The return was swift. In one hour the transformation was complete, and it was in that hour that the child developed the outward signs of the Blue Disease."

He paused. A murmur ran round the hall and then once more came silence.

85

"I am of the opinion," said Hammer deliberately, "that the cause of the miracle—for it was a miracle—was the Blue Disease. Think, Gentlemen, of a child in the last stages of septic peritonitis, practically dead. Think again of the same child, one hour later, alive, free from pain, smiling, interested—and stained with the Blue Disease. What conclusion, as honest men, are we to draw from that?"

He sat down. At once a man near him got to his feet.

"The point of view hinted at by the last speaker is correct," he said. "I can corroborate it to a small extent. This morning I was confined to my bed with the beginnings of a bad influenzal cold. At midday I developed the Blue Disease, and now I am as well as I have ever been in the whole of my life. I attribute my cure to the Blue Disease."

Scarcely had he taken his seat again when a grave scholarly man arose in the gallery.

"Gentlemen," he said, "I come from Birmingham; and it is a city of miracles. The sick are being cured in thousands daily. The hospitals are emptying daily. I verily believe that the Blue Disease may prove to be all that Dr. Sarakoff and Dr. Harden claim it to be."

The effect of these speakers upon the meeting was remarkable. A thrill passed over the crowded Hall. Hammer rose again.

"Let us accept for a moment that this new infection confers immortality on humanity," he said, weighing each word carefully. "What are we, as medical men, going to do? Look into the future—a future free from disease, from death, possibly from pain. Are we to accept such a future passively, or are we, as doctors, to strive to eradicate this new germ as we strive to eradicate other germs?"

Sir Jeremy Jones, with an expression of dismay, raised his hand.

"Surely, surely," he exclaimed shrilly, "we are going too far. That the Blue Disease may modify the course of illness is conceivable, and seems to be supported by evidence. But to assume that it confers immortality——"

"Why should we doubt it?" returned Hammer warmly. "We have been told that it does by two responsible men of science, and so far their claim is justified. You, Mr. Chairman, have not seen the miracle that I have seen this afternoon. If the germ can bring a moribund child back to life in an hour, why should it not banish disease from the world?"

"But if it does banish disease from the world, that does not

86

mean it confers immortality," objected Sir Jeremy. "Do you mean to say that we are to regard natural death as a disease?"

He gazed round the hall helplessly. Several men arose to speak, but were unable to obtain a hearing, for excitement now ran high and every man was discussing the situation with his neighbour. For a moment, a strange dread had gripped the meeting, paralysing thought, but it passed, and while some remained perplexed the majority began to resent vehemently the suggestions of Hammer. I could hear those immediately behind me insisting that the view was sheer rubbish. It was preposterous. It was pure lunacy. With these phrases, constantly repeated, they threw off the startling effect of Hammer's speech, and fortified themselves in the conviction that the Blue Disease was merely a new malady, similar to other maladies, and that life would proceed as before.

I turned to them.

"You are deliberately deceiving yourselves," I said. "You have heard the evidence. You are simply making as much noise as possible in order to shut out the truth."

My words enraged them. A sudden clamour arose around us. Several men shook their fists and there were angry cries. One of them made a movement towards us. In an instant calmness left us. The scene around us seemed to leap up to our senses as something terrible and dangerous. Sarakoff and I scrambled to our feet, pushed our way frantically through the throng, reached the corridor and dashed down it. Fear of indescribable intensity had flamed in our souls, and in a moment we found ourselves running violently down Regent Street.

CHAPTER XX

THE WAY BACK

It had been a wet night. Pools of water lay on the glistening pavements, but the rain had ceased. We ran steadily until we came in sight of Piccadilly Circus, and there our fear left us suddenly. It was like the cutting off of a switch. We stopped in the street, gasping for breath.

"This is really absurd," I observed; "we must learn to control ourselves."

"We can't control an emotion of that strength, Harden. It's overwhelming. It's all the emotion we had before concentrated into a single expression. No, it's going to be a nuisance."

"The worst of it is that we cannot foresee it. We get no warning. It springs out of the unknown like a tiger."

We walked slowly across the Circus. It was thronged with a night crowd, and seemed like some strange octagonal room, walled by moving coloured lights. Here lay a scene that remained eternally the same whatever the conditions of life—a scene that neither war, nor pestilence, nor famine could change. We stood by the fountain, immersed in our thoughts. "I used to enjoy this kind of thing," said Sarakoff at length.

"And now?"

"Now it is curiously meaningless—absolutely indecipherable."

We walked on and entered Coventry Street. Here Sarakoff suddenly pushed open a door and I followed him. We found ourselves in a brilliantly illuminated restaurant. A band was playing. We sat down at an unoccupied table.

"Harden, I wish to try an experiment. I want to see if, by an effort, we can get back to the old point of view."

He beckoned to the waiter and ordered champagne, cognac, oysters and caviare. Then he leaned back in his seat and smiled.

"Somehow I feel it won't work," I began.

He held up his hand.

"Wait. It is an experiment. You must give it a fair chance. Come, let us be merry."

I nodded.

"Let us eat, drink and be merry," I murmured.

I watched the flushed faces and sparkling eyes around us. So far we had attracted no attention. Our table was in a corner, behind a pillar. The waiter hurried up with a laden tray, and in a moment the table was covered with bottles and plates.

"Now," said Sarakoff, "we will begin with a glass of brandy. Let us try to recall the days of our youth—a little imagination, Harden, and then perhaps the spell will be broken. A toast—Leonora!"

"Leonora," I echoed.

We raised our glasses. I took a sip and set down my glass. Our eyes met.

"Is the brandy good?"

"It is of an admirable quality," said Sarakoff. He put his glass on the table and for some time we sat in silence.

"Excuse me," I said. "Don't you think the caviare is a trifle—?"

He made a gesture of determination.

"Harden, we will try champagne."

He filled two glasses.

"Let us drink off the whole glass," he said. "Really, Harden, we must try."

I managed to take two gulps. The stuff was nasty. It seemed like weak methylated spirits.

"Continue," said Sarakoff firmly; "let us drink ourselves into the glorious past, whither the wizard of alcohol transports all men."

I took two more gulps. Sarakoff did the same. It was something in the nature of a battle against an invisible resistance. I gripped the table hard with my free hand, and took another gulp.

"Sarakoff," I gasped. "I can't take any more. If you want to get alcohol into my system you must inject it under my skin. I can't do it this way."

He put down his glass. It was half full. There were beads of perspiration on his brow.

"I'll finish that glass somehow," he observed. He passed his hand across his forehead. "This is extraordinary. It's just like taking poison, Harden, and yet it is an excellent brand of wine."

"Do get these oysters taken away," I said. "They serve no purpose lying here. They only take up room."

"Wait till I finish my glass."

With infinite trouble he drank the rest of the champagne. The effort tired him. He sat, breathing quickly and staring before him.

"That's a pretty woman," he observed. "I did not notice her before."

I followed the direction of his gaze. A young woman, dressed in emerald green, sat at a table against the opposite wall. She was talking very excitedly, making many gestures and seemed to me a little intoxicated.

Sarakoff poured out some more champagne.

"I am getting back," he muttered. He looked like a man engaged in some terrific struggle with himself. His breath was short and thick, his eyes were reddened. Perspiration covered his face and hands. He finished the second glass.

"Yes, she is pretty," he said, "I like that white skin against the brilliant green. She's got grace, too. Have you noticed white-skinned women always are graceful, and have little ears, Harden?"

He laughed suddenly, with his old boisterousness and clapped me on the shoulder.

"This is the way out!" he shouted, and pointed to the silver tub that contained the champagne bottle.

His voice sounded loudly above the music.

"The way out!" he repeated. He got to his feet. His eyes were congested. The sweat streamed down his cheeks. "Here," he called in his deep powerful voice, "here, all you who are afraid—here is the way out." He waved his arms. People stopped drinking and talking to turn and stare at him. "Back to the animals!" he shouted. "Back to the fur and hair and flesh! I was up on the mountain top, but I've found the way back. Here it is—here is the magic you need, if you're tired of the frozen heights!"

He swayed as he spoke. Strangely interested, I stared up at him.

"He's delirious," called out the emerald young woman. "He's got that horrid disease."

The manager and a couple of waiters came up. "It's coming," shouted Sarakoff; "I saw it sweeping over the world. See, the world is white, like snow. They have robbed it of colour." The manager grasped his arm firmly.

"Come with me," he said. "You are ill. I will put you in a taxi."

"You don't understand," said Sarakoff. "You are in it still. Don't you see I'm a traveller?"

"He is mad," whispered a waiter in my ear.

"A traveller," shouted the Russian. "But I've come back. Greeting, brothers. It was a rough journey, but now I hear and see you."

"If you do not leave the establishment at once I will get a policeman," said the manager with a hiss.

Sarakoff threw out his hands.

"Make ready!" he cried. "The great uprooting!" He began to

laugh unsteadily. "The end of disease and the end of desire—there's no difference. You never knew that, brothers. I've come back to tell you—thousands and thousands of miles—into the great dimension of hell and heaven. It was a mistake and I'm going back. Look! She's fading—further and further——" He pointed a shaking hand across the room and suddenly collapsed, half supported by the manager.

"Dead drunk," remarked a neighbour.

I turned.

"No. Live drunk," I said. "The champagne has brought him back to the world of desire."

The speaker, a clean-shaven young man, stared insolently.

"You have no business to come into a public place with that disease," he said with a sneer.

"You are right. I have no business here. My business is to warn the world that the end of desire is at hand." I signalled to a waiter and together we managed to get Sarakoff into a taxi-cab.

As we drove home, all that lay behind Sarakoff's broken confused words revealed itself with increasing distinctness to me.

Sarakoff spoke again.

"Harden," he muttered thickly, "there was a flaw—in the dream——"

"Yes," I said. "I was sure there would be a flaw. I hadn't noticed it before——"

"We're cut off," he whispered. "Cut off."

CHAPTER XXI

JASON

Next morning the headlines of the newspapers blazed out the news of the meeting at the Queen's Hall, and the world read the words of Sarakoff.

Strange to say, most of the papers seemed inclined to view the situation seriously.

"If," said one in a leading article, "it really means that immortality is coming to humanity—and there is, at least, much evidence from Birmingham that supports the view that the germ cures all sickness—then we are indeed face to face with a strange problem. For how will immortality affect us as a community? As a community, we live together on the tacit assumption that the old will die and the young will take their place. All our laws and customs are based on this idea. We can scarcely think of any institution that is not established upon the certainty of death. What, then, if death ceases? Our food supply——"

I was interrupted, while reading, by my servant who announced that a gentleman wished to see me on urgent business. I laid aside the paper and waited for him to enter.

My early visitor was a tall, heavily-built man, with strong eyes. He was carefully dressed. He looked at me attentively, nodded, and sat down.

"My name is Jason—Edward Jason. You have no doubt heard of me."

"Certainly," I said. "You are the proprietor of this paper that I have just been reading."

He nodded.

"And of sixty other daily papers, Dr. Harden," he said in a soft voice. "I control much of the opinion in the country, and I intend to control it all before I die."

"A curious intention. But why should you die? You will get the germ in time. I calculate that in a month at the outside the whole of London and the best part of the country will be infected."

While I spoke he stared hard at me. He nodded again, glanced at his boots, pinched his lips, and then stared again.

"A year ago I made a tour of all the big men in your profession, both here, in America, and on the continent, Dr.

Harden. I had a very definite reason for doing this. The reason was that—well, it does not matter now. I wanted a diagnosis and a forecast of the future. I consulted forty medical men—all with big names. Twenty-one gave me practically identical opinions. The remaining nineteen were in disagreement. Of that nineteen six gave me a long life."

"What did the twenty-one give you?"

"Five years at the outside."

I looked at him critically.

"Yes, I should have given the same—a year ago."

He coloured a little, and his gaze fell; he shifted himself in his chair. Then he looked up suddenly, with a strong glow in his eyes.

"And now?"

"Now I give you—immortality." I spoke quite calmly, with no intention of any dramatic effect.

The colour faded from his cheeks, and the glow in his eyes increased.

"If I get the Blue Disease, do you swear that it will cure me?"

"Of course it will cure you."

He got to his feet. He seemed to be in the grip of some powerful emotion, and I could see that he was determined to control himself. He walked down the room and stood for some time near the window.

"A gipsy once told me I would die when I was fifty-two. Will you believe me when I say that that prophecy has weighed upon me more than any medical opinion?" He turned and came up the room and stood before me. "Did you ever read German psychology and philosophy?"

"To a certain extent—in translations."

"Well, Dr. Harden, I stepped out of the pages of some of those books, I think. You've heard of the theory of the Will to Power? The men who based human life on that instinct were right!" He clenched his hands and closed his eyes. "This last year has been hell to me. I've been haunted every hour by the thought of death—just so much longer—so many thousand days—and then Nothing!" He opened his eyes and sat down before me. "Are you ambitious, Dr. Harden?"

"I was—very ambitious."

"Do you know what it is to have a dream of power, luring you on day and night? Do you know what is to see the dream becoming reality, bit by bit—and then to be given a time limit, when the dream is only half worked out?"

"I have had my dream," I said. "It is now realized."

"The germ?"

93

I nodded. He leaned forward.

"Then you are satisfied?"

"I have no desires now."

He did not appear to understand.

"I don't believe yet in your theory of immortality," he said slowly. "But I do believe that the germ cures sickness. I have had private reports from Birmingham, and to-morrow I'm going to publish them as evidence. You see, Harden, I've decided to back you. To-morrow I'm going to make Gods of you and your Russian associate. I'm going to call you the greatest benefactors the race has known. I'm going to lift you up to the skies."

He looked at me earnestly.

"Doesn't that stir you?" he asked.

"No, I told you that I have no desires."

He laughed.

"You're dazed. You must have worked incredibly hard. Wait till you see your name surrounded by the phrases I will devise you. I can make men out of nothing." His eyes shone into mine. "I once heard a man say that the trail of the serpent lay across my papers. That man is in an asylum now. I can break men, too, you see. Now I want to ask you something."

I watched him with ease, totally uninfluenced by his magnetism—calm and aloof as a man watching a mechanical doll.

"Can you limit the germ?" he asked softly.

I shook my head.

"Can you take any steps to stop it or keep it—within control?"

I shook my head again. He stared for a minute at me.

"I believe you," he said at last. "It's a pity. Think what we could have done—just a few of us!" He sat for some time drumming his fingers on his knees and frowning slightly. Then he stood up.

"Never mind," he exclaimed. "I'm convinced it will cure me. That is the main thing. I'll have plenty of time to realize my dream now, Harden, thanks to you. You don't know what that means—ah, you don't know!"

"By the way," I said, "I see you are suggesting that food may become a problem in the future. I think we'll be all right."

"Why?"

"Well, you see, if there's no desire, there's no appetite."

"I don't understand," he said. "It seems clear that if disease is mastered by the germ, then the death-rate will drop, and there will be more mouths to fill. If everyone lives for their threescore and ten, the food question will be serious."

"Oh, they'll live longer than that. They'll live for ever, Mr. Jason."

He laughed tolerantly.

"In any case there will be a food problem," he said in a quiet friendly voice. "There will be more births, and more children—for none will die—and more old people."

"There won't be more births," I said.

He swung round on his heel.

"Why not?" he asked sharply.

"Because there will be no desire, Mr. Jason. You can't have births without desires, don't you see?"

At that moment Sarakoff entered the room. I introduced him to the great newspaper proprietor. Jason made some complimentary remarks, which Sarakoff received with cool gravity.

I could see that Jason was very puzzled. He had seated himself again, and was watching the Russian closely.

"The effects of last night have vanished," said Sarakoff to me. "My head is clear again and I have no intention of ever repeating the experiment."

"You got back, to some extent."

"Yes, partly. It was tremendously painful. I felt like a man in a nightmare."

I turned to Jason and explained what had happened at the restaurant. He listened intently.

"You see," I concluded, "the germ kills desire. Sarakoff and I live on a level of consciousness that is undisturbed by any craving. We live in a wonderful state of peace, which is only broken by the appearance of physical danger—against which, of course, the germ is not proof."

Jason was silent.

"Do you mean to tell me," he said at length, in a very deliberate voice, "that the effect of the germ is to destroy ambition?"

"Worldly ambition, certainly," I replied. "But I believe that, in time, ambitions of a subtler nature will reveal themselves in us, as Immortals."

Jason smiled very broadly.

"Gentlemen," he said, "you are wonderful men. You have discovered something that benefits humanity enormously. But take my advice—leave your other theories alone. Stick to the facts—that your germ cures sickness. Drop the talk about immortality and desire. It's too fantastic, even for me. In the meantime I shall spread abroad the news that the end of sickness is at hand, and that

95

humanity is on the threshold of a new era. For that I believe with all my heart."

"One moment," said Sarakoff. "If you believe that this germ does away with disease, what is going to cause men to die?"

"Old age."

"But that is a disease itself."

"Wear and tear isn't a disease. That's what kills most of us."

"Yes, but wear and tear comes from desire, Mr. Jason," I said. "And the germ knocks that out. So what is left, save immortality?"

When Jason left us, I could see that he was impressed by the possibility of life being, at least, greatly prolonged. And this was the line he took in his newspapers next day.

CHAPTER XXII

THE FIRST MURDERS

The effect of Jason's newspapers on public opinion was remarkable. Humanity ever contains within it the need for mystery, and the strange and incredible, if voiced by authority, stir it to its depths. The facts about the healing of sickness and the cure of disease in Birmingham were printed in heavy type and read by millions. Nothing was said about immortality save what Sarakoff and I had stated at the Queen's Hall meeting. But instinctively the multitude leaped to the conclusion that if the end of disease was at hand, then the end of death—at least, the postponement of death—was to be expected.

Jason, pale and masterful, visited us in the afternoon, and told us of the spread of the tidings in England. "They've swallowed it," he exclaimed; "it's stirred them as nothing else has done in the last hundred years. I visited the East End to-day. The streets are full of people. Crowds everywhere. It might lead to anything."

"Is the infection spreading swiftly?"

"It's spreading. But there are plenty of people, like myself, who haven't got it yet. I should say that a quarter of London is blue." He looked at me with a sudden anxiety. "You're sure I'll get it?"

"Quite sure. Everyone is bound to get it. There's no possible immunity."

He sat heavily in the chair, staring at the carpet.

"Harden, I didn't quite like the look of those crowds in the East End. Anything big like this stirs up the people. It excites them and then the incalculable may happen. I've been thinking about the effect upon the uneducated mind. I've spread over the country the vision of humanity free from disease, and that's roused something in them—something dangerous—that I didn't foresee. Disease, Harden, whatever you doctors think of it, puts the fear of God into humanity. It's these sudden releases—releases from ancient fears—that are so dangerous. Are you sure you can't stop the germ, or direct it along certain channels?"

"I have already told you that's impossible."

"You might as well try and stop the light of day," said Sarakoff from a sofa, where he was lying apparently asleep. "Let the people think what they like now. Wait till they get it themselves. There are rules in the game, Jason, that you have no conception of, and that I have only realized since I became immortal. Yes—rules in the game, whether you play it in the cellar or the attic, or in the valley, or on the mountain top."

"Your friend is very Russian," said Jason equably. "I have always heard they are dreamers and visionaries. Personally, I am a practical man, and as such I foresee trouble. If the masses of the people have no illness, and enjoy perfect health, we shall be faced by a difficult problem. They'll get out of hand. Depressed states of health are valuable assets in keeping the social organization together. All this demands careful thought. I am visiting the Prime Minister this evening and shall give him my views."

At that moment a newspaper boy passed the window with an afternoon edition and Jason went out to get a copy. He returned with a smile of satisfaction, carrying the paper open before him.

"Three murders in London," he announced. "One in Plaistow, one in East Ham and one in Pimlico. I told you there was unrest abroad." He laid the paper on the table and studied it "In every case it was an aged person—two old women, and one old man. Now what does that mean?"

"A gang at work."

He shook his head.

"No. In one case the murderer has been caught. It was a case of patricide—a hideous crime. Curiously enough the victim had the Blue Disease. The end must have been ghastly, as it states here that the expression on the old man's face was terrible."

He sat beside the table, drumming his fingers on it and staring at the wall before him. I was not particularly interested in the news, but I was interested in Jason. Character had formerly appealed little to me, but now I found an absorbing problem in it.

"Harden, do you think that son killed his father because he had the Blue Disease?"

I was struck by the remark. For somereason the picture of Alice's father came into my mind. Jason sprang to his feet.

"Yes, that's it," he exclaimed. "That's what lay behind those restless crowds. I knew there was something—a riddle to read, and now I've got the answer. The crowd doesn't know what's rousing them. But I do. It's fear and resentment, Harden. It's fear and resentment against the old." He brought his fist down on the table. "The germ's going to lead to war! It's going to lead to the worst war humanity has ever experienced—the war of the young against the old. Not the ancient strife or struggle between young and old, but open bloodshed, my friends. That's what your germ is going to do."

I smiled and shook my head.

"Wait," said Sarakoff from the sofa; "wait a little. Why are you in such a hurry to jump to conclusions?"

"Because it's my business to jump to conclusions just six hours before anyone else does," said Jason. "I calculate that my mind, for the last twenty years, has been six hours ahead of time. I live in a state of chronic anticipation, Dr. Sarakoff. Just let me use your telephone for a moment."

He returned a quarter of an hour later. His expression was calm, but his eyes were hard. "I was right," he said. "Those two old women had the Blue Disease, and a girl, a daughter, is suspect in one case. Can't you imagine the situation? Girl lives with her aged mother—can't get free—mother has what money there is—not allowed to marry—girl unconsciously counts on mother's death—probably got a secret love-affair—is expecting the moment of release—and then, along comes the Blue Disease and one of my newspapers telling her what it means. The old lady recovers her health—the future shuts down like a rat trap and what does the poor girl do? Kills her mother—and probably goes mad. That, gentlemen, is my theory of the case."

He strode up and down the room.

"You may think I'm taking a low view," he cried. "But there are hundreds of thousands of similar cases in England. God help the old if the young forget their religion!"

For some reason I was unmoved by the outcry. It was no doubt owing to the peculiar emotionless state that the germ induced in people. Jason was roused. He paced to and fro in silence, with his brows contracted. At length he stopped before me.

"Do you see any way out?"

"There will be no war between the young and the old," I replied. "In another week everyone will get the germ and that will be the end of war in every form."

He drew a chair and sat down before me.

"You don't understand," he said earnestly. "Perhaps you had a happy childhood. I didn't. I know how some sons and daughters feel because I suffered in that way. People are strangely blind to suffering unless they have suffered themselves. When I was a young man, my father put me in his office and gave me a clerk's wages. He kept me there for six years at eighteen shillings a week. Whenever I made a suggestion concerning the business he was careful to ridicule it. Whenever I tried to break away and start on my own, he prevented it. There were a thousand other things—ways in which he fettered me. My only sister he kept at home to do the housework. He forbade her to marry. She and I never had enough money to do anything, to go anywhere, or to buy anything. Now, to be quite

99

frank, I longed for him to die so that I could get free. To me he was an ogre, a great merciless tyrant, a giant with a club. Well, he died. When he was dead I felt what a man dying of thirst in the desert must feel when he suddenly comes to a spring of water. I recovered, and became what I am. My sister never recovered. She had been suppressed beyond all the limits of elasticity. As far as her body is concerned, it is alive. Her soul is dead."

He paused and looked at me meditatively.

"If your blue germ had come along then, Harden, I might—— Who knows? I have often wondered why our pulpit religion ignores the crimes of parents to their children. I'm not conventionally religious, but I seem to remember that Christ indirectly said something pretty strong on the subject. But the pulpit folk show a wonderful facility for ignoring the awkward things Christ said. In about three years' time I'm going to turn my guns on the Church. They've sneered at me too much."

"There will be a new Church by that time," murmured Sarakoff. "And no guns."

Jason eyed the prostrate figure of the Russian.

"I refer to my newspapers. That's going to be my final triumph. Why do you smile?"

"Because you said a moment ago that it was your business to be six hours ahead of everyone else. You're countless centuries behind Harden and me. We have taken a leap into the future. If you want to know what humanity will be, look at us closely. You'll get some hints that should be valuable. I admit that our bodies are old-fashioned in their size and shape, but not our emotions."

The telephone bell rang in the hall and Jason jumped up.

"I think that's for me."

He went out. I remained sitting calmly in my chair. An absolute serenity surrounded me. All that Jason did or said was like looking at an interesting play. I was perfectly content to sit and think—think of Jason, of what his motives were, of the reason why a man is blind where his desires are at work, of the new life, of the new organizations that would be necessary. I was like a glutton before a table piled high with delicacies and with plenty of time to spare. Sarakoff seemed to be in the same condition for he lay with his eyes half shut, motionless and absorbed.

Jason entered the room suddenly. He carried his hat and stick.

"Two more murders reported from Greenwich, and ten from Birmingham. It's becoming serious, Harden! I'm off to Downing Street. Watch the morning editions!"

CHAPTER XXIII

AT DOWNING STREET

That night, at eight o'clock, I was summoned to Downing Street. I left Sarakoff lying on the sofa, apparently asleep. I drove the first part of the way in a taxi, but at the corner of Orchard Street the cab very nearly collided with another vehicle, and in a moment I was a helpless creature of fear. So I walked the rest of the way, much to the astonishment of the driver, who thought I was a lunatic. It was a fine crisp evening and the streets were unusually full. Late editions of the paper were still being cried, and under the lamps were groups of people, talking excitedly.

From what I could gather from snatches of conversation that I overheard, it seemed that many thought the millennium was at hand. I mused on this, wondering if beneath the busy exterior of life there lurked in people's hearts a secret imperishable conviction. And, after all, was it not a millennium—the final triumph of science—the conquest of the irrational by the rational?

There was a good deal of drunkenness, and crowds of men and women, linked arm and arm, went by, singing senseless songs. In Piccadilly Circus the scene was unusually animated. Here, beyond doubt, the Jason press had produced a powerful impression. The restaurants and bars blazed with light. Crowds streamed in and out and a spirit of hilarious excitement pervaded everyone. Irresponsibility—that was the universal attitude; and I became deeply occupied in thinking how the germ should have brought about such a temper in the multitude. Only occasionally did I catch the blue stain in the eyes of the throng about me.

I reached Downing Street and was shown straight into a large, rather bare room. By the fireplace sat Jason, and beside him, on the hearthrug, stood the Premier. Jason introduced me and I was greeted with quiet courtesy.

"I intend to make a statement in the House to-night and would like to put a few questions to you," said the Premier in a slow clear voice. "The Home Secretary has been considering whether you and Dr. Sarakoff should be arrested. I see no use in that. What you have done cannot be undone."

"That is true."

"In matters like this," he continued, "it is always a question of

101

taking sides. Either we must oppose you and the germ, or we must side with you, and extol the virtues of the new discovery. A neutral attitude would only rouse irritation. I have therefore looked into the evidence connected with the effects claimed for the germ, and have received reports on the rate of its spread. It would seem that it is of benefit to man, so far as can be judged at present, and that its course cannot be stayed."

I assented, and remained gazing abstractedly at the fire.

He continued in a sterner tone—

"It may, however, be necessary to place you and Dr. Sarakoff under police protection. There is no saying what may happen. Your action in letting loose the germ in the water supply of Birmingham was unfortunate. You have taken a great liberty with humanity, whatever may result from it."

"Medical men have no sense of proportion," murmured Jason. "Science makes them so helpless."

"I see no kind of helplessness in rescuing humanity from disease," I answered calmly. "Please tell me what you want to know."

They both looked at me attentively. The Premier took out a pair of pince-nez and began to clean the lenses, still watching me.

"France is unwilling to let the germ into her territory. Can measures be taken to stop its access to the Continent?"

"No. It will get there inevitably. It has probably got there long ago. It is air borne and water borne and probably sea borne as well. The whole world will be infected sooner or later. There is no immunity possible."

The Premier put on his pince-nez and warmed his hands at the fire.

"Then what will the result of the germ be upon mankind?" he asked at length.

"It will begin a new era. What has made reform so difficult up to now?"

"People do not see eye to eye on all questions, Dr. Harden. That is the main reason."

"And why do they not see eye to eye?"

"Because their desires are not the same."

"Very good. Now imagine a humanity without desires, as you and Jason understand desire. What would be the result?"

"It is impossible to conceive. The wheels of the world would cease turning. We should be like sheep without a shepherd." He surveyed me quietly for some time. "Then you think the germ will kill desire?"

102

"I know it. I am a living example. I have no desires. I am like a man without a body, I am immortal."

Jason laughed.

"You are above temptation?" he asked.

"Absolutely. Neither money, power nor woman has any influence on me. They are meaningless."

"You have, perhaps, reached Nirvana?" the Premier enquired.

"Yes. That is why I am immortal. I have reached Nirvana."

"By a trick."

"If you like—by a trick."

"Then I cannot think you will stay there for long," said the Premier. "I shall look forward to my attack of the Blue Disease with interest. It will be amusing to note one's sensations."

It was clear to me that he was defending himself against my greater knowledge, but it was a matter of no importance to me. I was faintly oppressed by the dreary immensity of the room. I had become sensitive to atmosphere, and the feeling of that room was not harmonious.

The Premier stood in deep thought.

"If the germ prolongs life, it will lead to complications," he remarked. "The question of being too old has attracted public attention for some time now, which shows the way the wind is blowing. Oldness has become, in a small degree, a problem. The world is younger than it used to be—more impatient, more anxious to live a free life, to escape from any form of bondage. And so people have begun to ask what we are to do with our old men."

He paused and looked at Jason.

"My friend Jason thinks these murders are caused indirectly by the germ."

"It is possible."

"It seems fantastic. But there may be something in it." The Premier raised his eyes and studied the ceiling. "There is certainly some excitement abroad. We are dealing with an unprecedented situation. I therefore propose to say to-night that if, in the course of time, we find that life is prolonged and disease done away with, new laws will have to be considered."

"Not only new laws," I said. "We shall have to reconstruct the whole future of life. But there is no hurry. There is plenty of time. There is eternity before us."

"What do you eat?" demanded the Premier suddenly.

"A little bread or biscuit."

He clasped his hands behind his back and surveyed me for quite a minute.

103

"I don't believe you're a quack," he observed. "But when you walked into the room, I was doubtful."

"Why?"

"Because you wouldn't look at me squarely."

"Why should I look at you squarely? I looked at you and saw you. I have no desire to make any impression on you, or to dominate you in any way. It was sufficient just to see you. As Immortals, we do not waste our time looking at one another squarely. An Immortal cannot act."

The Premier smiled to himself and took out his watch.

"I am obliged to you for the instance," he said. "Good-night."

I rose and walked towards the door. On my way I stopped before a vast dingy oil-painting.

"Why do you all deceive yourselves that you admire things like that? Throw it away. When you become an Immortal you won't live here."

The Premier and Jason stood together on the hearth-rug. They watched me intently as I went out and closed the door behind me. A servant met me on the landing and escorted me downstairs. I observed that he was an Immortal.

"What are you doing here?" I asked.

"I am a spectator," he said in a calm voice. "And you?"

"I, too, am a spectator."

CHAPTER XXIV

NIGHT OF AN IMMORTAL

I passed a most remarkable night. On reaching home I went to bed as usual. My mind was busy, but what busied it was not the events of the day.

I lay in the darkness in a state of absolute contentment. My eyes were closed. My body was motionless, and felt warm and comfortable. I was quite aware of the position of my limbs in space and I could hear the sound of passing vehicles outside. I was not asleep and yet at the same time I was not awake. I knew I was not properly awake because, when I tried to move, there seemed to be a resistance to the impulse, which prevented it from reaching the muscles. As I have already said, I could feel. The sensation of my body was there, though probably diminished, but the power of movement was checked, though only slightly. And all the time I lay in that state, my mind was perfectly lucid and continually active. I thought about many things and the power of thought was very great, in that I could keep my attention fixed hour after hour on the same train of thought, go backwards and forwards along it, change and modify its gradations, just as if I were dealing with some material and plastic formation. Since that time I have become acquainted with a doctrine that teaches that thoughts are in the nature of things—that a definite thought is a formation in some tenuous medium of matter, just as a cathedral is a structure in gross matter. This is certainly the kind of impression I gained then.

It was now in the light of contrast that I could reflect on the rusty and clumsy way in which I had previously done my thinking, and I remembered with a faint amusement that there had been a time when I considered that I had a very clear and logical mind. Logical! What did we, as mere mortals full of personal desire, know of logic? The reflection seemed infinitely humorous. My thoughts had about them a new quality of stability. They formed themselves into clear images, which had a remarkable permanence. Their power and influence was greatly increased. If, for example, I thought out a bungalow situated on the cliff, I built up, piece by piece in my mind, the complete picture; and once built up it remained there so that I could see it as a whole, and almost, so to speak, walk round it and view it from different angles. I could lay aside this thought-creation just as I might lay aside a model in clay, and later on bring it back into my mind, as fresh and clear as ever. The enjoyment of thinking under such conditions is impossible to describe. It was like the joy of a man, blind from childhood, suddenly receiving his sight.

As ordinary mortals, we are all familiar with the apparently real scenes that occur in dreams. In our dreams we see buildings and walk round them. We see flights of steps and climb them. We apparently touch and taste food. We meet friends and strangers and converse with them. At times we seem to gaze over landscapes covered with woods and meadows.

It seemed to me that the magic of dreams had in some way become attached to thought. For as Immortals we did not dream as mortals do. In place of dreaming, we created immense thought-forms, working as it were on a new plane of matter whose resources were inexhaustible.

That night I built my ideal bungalow and when I had finished it I constructed my ideal garden. And then I made a sea and a coast-line, and when it was finished it was so real to me that I actually seemed to go into its rooms, sit on the verandah, breathe in its sea-airs and listen to the surf below its cliff. I remember that one of its rooms did not please me entirely, and that I seemed to pull it down—in thought—and reconstruct it according to my wish. This took time, for brick by brick I thought the new room into existence. One law that governed that state was easy to grasp, for whatever you did not think out clearly assumed a blurred unsatisfactory form. It became clear to me as early as that first night of immortality that the more familiar a man was with matter on the earth and its ways and possibilities, the more easily could he make his constructions on that plan of thought.

The whole of that night I lay in this state of creative joy and I know that my body remained motionless. It seemed that only a film divided me from the use of my limbs, but that film was definite. At eight o'clock on that morning, I became aware of a vague feeling of strain. It was a very slight sensation, but its effect was to make the thoughts that occupied my consciousness to become less definite. I had to make an effort to keep them distinct. The strain slowly became greater. It had begun with a sense of distance, but it seemed to get nearer, and I experienced a feeling that I can only compare to as that which a man has when he is losing his balance and about to fall.

The strain ended suddenly. I found myself moving my limbs. I opened my eyes and looked round. The graphic, visible quality of my thoughts had now vanished. I was awake.

I have given the above account of the night of an Immortal, because it has seemed to me right that some record should be left of the effect of the germ on the mind. I would explain the inherent power of thought as being due to the freedom from the ordinary desires of mortals, which waste and dissipate the energies of the mind ... but of that I cannot be certain.

CHAPTER XXV

OUR FLIGHT

I got out of bed and began to examine my clothes. They were strewn about the floor and on chairs. The colour of them seemed peculiar to my senses. My frock coat, of heavy black material, with curious braiding and buttons, fascinated me. I counted the number of separate things that made up my complete attire. They were twenty-four in number. I discovered that in addition to these articles of actual wearing material I was in the habit of carrying on my person about sixty other articles. For some reason I found these calculations very interesting. I had a kind of counting mania that morning. I counted all the things I used in dressing myself. I counted the number of stripes on my trousers and on my wall-paper; I counted the number of rooms in my house, thearticles of furniture that they contained, and the number of electric lamps. I went into the kitchen and counted everything I could see, to the astonishment of my servants. I observed that my cook showed a faint blue stain in her eyes, but that the other servants showed no signs as yet of the Blue Disease. I went into my study and counted the books; I opened one of them. It was the British Pharmacopœia. I began mechanically to count the number of drugs it contained. I was still counting them when the breakfast gong sounded. I went across the hall and counted on my way the number of sticks and hats and coats that were there. I finished up by counting the number of things on the breakfast table. Then I picked up the newspaper. There were, by the way, one hundred and four distinct things on my breakfast table.

The paper was full of the records of crime and of our names.

The account of the Prime Minister's statement in the House was given in full. Our names were printed in large letters, and apparently our qualifications had been looked up, for they were mentioned, together with a little biographical sketch. In a perfectly calm and observant spirit I read the closely-printed column. My eye paused for some time at an account of my personal appearance—"a small, insignificant-looking man, with straight blue-black hair, like a Japanese doll, and an untidy moustache, speaking very deliberately and with a manner of extreme self-assurance."

Extreme self-assurance! I reflected that there might, after all, be some truth in what the reporter said. On the night that I had spoken at the Queen's Hall meeting I had been quite self-possessed. I pursued the narrative and smiled slightly at a description of the Russian—"a loosely-built, bearded giant, unkempt in appearance, and with huge square hands and pale Mongolian eyes which roll like those of a maniac." That was certainly unfair, unless the reporter had seen him at the restaurant when Sarakoff drank the champagne. I was about to continue, when a red brick suddenly landed neatly on my breakfast table, and raised the number of articles on that table to one hundred and five.

There was a tinkle of falling glass; I looked up and saw that the window was shattered. The muslin curtain in front of it had been torn down by the passage of the brick, and the street without was visible from where I sat. A considerable crowd had gathered on the pavement. They saw me and a loud cry went up. The front door bell was ringing and there was a sound of heavy blows that echoed through the house.

My housemaid came running into the room. She uttered a shriek as she saw the faces beyond the window and ran out again. I heard a door at the back of the house slam suddenly.

A couple of men, decently enough dressed, were getting over the area rails with the intent of climbing in at the window. I jumped up and went swiftly upstairs. So far I was calm. I entered Sarakoff's bedroom. It was in darkness. The Russian was lying motionless on the bed. I shook him by the shoulder. It seemed impossible to rouse him, and yet in outward appearance he seemed only lightly asleep. I redoubled my efforts and at length he opened his eyes, and his whole body, which had felt under my hands as limp and flaccid as a pillow, suddenly seemed to tighten up and become resilient.

"Get up," I said. "They're trying to break into the house. We may be in danger. We can escape by the back door through the mews."

The blows on the front door were clearly audible.

"I've been listening to it for some time," he said. "But I seemed to have lost the knack of waking up properly."

"We have no time to waste," I said firmly.

We went quickly downstairs. Sarakoff had flung a blue dressing-gown over his pyjamas and thrust his feet into a pair of slippers. On reaching the hall there was a loud crack and a roar of voices. In an instant the agonizing fear swept over us. We dashed to the back of the house, through the servants' quarters and out into the mews. Without pausing for an instant we ran down the cobbled alley and emerged upon Devonshire Street. We turned to the right, dashed across Portland Place and reached Great Portland Street. We ran steadily, wholly mastered by the great fear of physical injury, and oblivious to the people around us. We passed the Underground Station. Our flight down the Euston Road was extraordinary. Sarakoff was in front, his dressing-gown flying, and his pink pyjamas making a vivid area of colour in the drab street. I followed a few yards in the rear, hatless, with my breath coming in gasps.

It was Sarakoff who first saw the taxi-cab. He veered suddenly into the road and held out his arms. The cab slowed down and in a moment we were inside it.

"Go on," shouted Sarakoff, "Drive on. Don't stop."

The driver was a man of spirit and needed no further directions. The cab jerked forward and we sped towards St. Pancras Station.

"Follow the tram lines up to Hampstead," I called out, and he nodded. We lay gasping in the back of the cab, cannoning helplessly as it swayed round corners. By the time we had reached Hampstead our fear had left us.

The cab drew up on the Spaniard's Walk and we alighted. It was a bleak and misty morning. The road seemed deserted. A thin column of steam rose from the radiator of the taxi, and there was a smell of over-heated oil.

"Sharp work that," said the driver, getting out and beating his arms across his chest. His eyes moved over us with frank curiosity. Sarakoff shivered and drew his dressing-gown closely round him.

CHAPTER XXVI

ON THE SPANIARD'S WALK

I paid the man half-a-sovereign. There was a seat near by and Sarakoff deposited himself upon it. I joined him. On those heights the morning air struck chill. London, misty-blue, lay before us. The taxi-man took out his pipe and began to fill it.

"Lucky me comin' along like that," he observed. "If it hadn't been because of my missus I wouldn't have been out so early." He blew a puff of smoke and continued: "This Blue Disease seems to confuse folk. My missus was took with it last night." He paused to examine us at his leisure. "When did you get it?"

"We became immortal the day before yesterday," said Sarakoff.

The taxi-man took his pipe out of his mouth and stared.

"You ain't them two doctors what's in the paper this morning, by any chance?" he asked. "Them as is supposed to 'ave invented this Blue Disease?"

We nodded. He emitted a low whistle and gazed thoughtfully at us. At length he spoke I noticed his tone had changed.

"As I was saying, my missus was took with it in the night. I had a job waking 'er up, and when she opened her eyes I near had a fit. We'd had a bit of a tiff overnight, but she got up as quiet as a lamb and never said a word agin me, which surprised me. When I 'ad dressed myself I went into the kitchen to get a bit o' breakfast, and she was setting in a chair starin' at nothing. The kettle wasn't boiling, and there wasn't nothing ready, so I asked 'er quite polite, what she was doing. 'I'm thinking,' she says, and continues sitting in the chair. After a bit of reasoning with her, I lost my temper and picked up a leg of a chair, what we had broke the evening previous when we was 'aving a argument. She jump up and bolted out of the house, just as she was, with her 'air in curl-papers, and that's the last I saw of her. I waited an hour and then took the old cab out of the garage, and I was going to look for my breakfast when I met you two gents." He took his pipe out of his mouth and wiped his lips. "Now I put it all down to this 'ere Blue Disease. It's sent my missus off 'er head."

"There's no reason why you should think your wife mad simply because she ran away when you tried to strike her," I said. "It's surely a proof of her sanity."

He shook his head.

"That ain't correct," he said, with conviction. "She always liked a scrap. She's a powerful young woman, and her language is extraordinary fine when she's roused, and she knows it. I can't understand it."

He looked up suddenly.

"So it was you two who made this disease was it?"

"Yes."

"Fancy that!" he said. "Fancy a couple of doctors inventing a disease. It does sound a shame, don't it?"

"Wait till you get it," said Sarakoff.

"It seems to me you've been and done something nasty," he went on. "Ain't there enough diseases without you two going and makin' a new one? It's a fair sickener to think of all the diseases there are—measles and softenin' of the brain, and 'eaving stummicks and what not. What made you do it? That's what I want to know." He was getting angry. He pointed the stem of his pipe at us accusingly. His small eyes shone. "It's fair sickening," he muttered. "I've never took to doctors, nor parsons—never in my life."

He spat expressively.

"And my wife, too, clean barmy," he continued. "Who 'ave I got to thank for that? You two gents. Doctors, you call yourselves. I arsk you, what is doctors? They never does me any good. I never seed anyone they'd done any good. And yet they keeps on and no one says nothing. It's fair sickening."

There was a sound of footsteps behind me. I turned and saw a policeman climbing slowly up the bank towards the road. Like all policemen he appeared not to notice us until he was abreast of our seat. Then he stopped and eyed each of us in turn. His boots were muddy.

"These gents," said the taxi-man, "'ave been and done something nasty."

The phrase seemed attractive to him and herepeated it. The policeman, a tall muscular man, surveyed us in silence. Sarakoff, his hair and beard dishevelled, was leaning back in a corner of the seat, with his legs crossed. His dressing-gown was tucked closely round him, and below it, his pink pyjamas fluttered in the thin breeze. His expression was calm.

The taxi-man continued—

"I picked these gents up in the Euston Road. They was in a hurry. I thought they'd done something ordinary, same as what you or me might do, but it seems I was wrong. They've been and done something nasty. They've gone and invented this 'ere Blue Disease."

The policeman raised his helmet a little and the taxi-man uttered an exclamation.

"Why, you've got it yourself," he said, and stared. The policeman's eyes were stained a vivid blue.

"An immortal policeman!" murmured Sarakoff dreamily.

The discovery seemed to discomfit the taxi-man. The tide of indignation in him was deflected, and he shifted his feet. The policeman, with a deliberation that was magnificent advanced to the seat and sat down beside me.

"Good-morning," I said.

"Good-morning," he replied in a deep calm voice. He removed his helmet from his head and allowed the wind to stir his hair. The taxi-man moved a step nearer us.

"You ought to arrest them," he said. "Here's my wife got it, and you, and who's to say when it will end? They're doctors, too. I allus had my own suspicions of doctors, and 'ere they are, just as I supposed, inventing diseases to keep themselves going. That's what you ought to do ... arrest them. I'll drive you all down to the police-station." The policeman replaced his helmet, crossed his long blue legs, and leaned back in the corner of the seat. Side by side on the seat Sarakoff, the policeman, and I gazed tranquilly at the figure of the taxi-man, at the taxi-cab, and at the misty panorama of London that lay beyond the Vale of Health. The expression of anger returned to the taxi-man's face.

"And 'ere am I, standing and telling you to do your duty, and all the time I haven't had my breakfast," he said bitterly. "If you was to cop them two gents, your name would be in all the evenin' papers." He paused, and frowned, conscious that he was making little impression on the upholder of law and order. "Why 'aven't I 'ad my breakfast? All because of these two blokes. I tell you, you ought to cop them."

"When I was a boy," said the policeman, "I used to collect stamps."

"Did yer," exclaimed the taxi-man sarcastically. "You do interest me, reely you do."

"Yes, I used to collect stamps." The policeman settled himself more comfortably. "And afore that I was in the 'abit of collecting bits o' string."

"You surprise me," said the taxi-man. "And what did you collect afore you collected bits of string?"

"So far as I recollect, I didn't collect nothing. I was trying to remember while I was walking across the Heath." He turned to us. "Did you collect anything?"

"Yes," I said. "I used to collect beetles."

"Beetles?" The policeman nodded thoughtfully. "I never had an eye for beetles. But, as I said, I collected stamps. I remember I would walk for miles to get a new stamp, and of an evening I would sit and count the stamps in my album over and over again till my head was fair giddy." He paused and stroked his clean-shaven chin thoughtfully. "I recollect as if it was yesterday how giddy my head used to get."

The taxi-man seemed about to say something, but he changed his mind.

"Why did you collect beetles?" the policeman asked me.

"I was interested in them."

"But that ain't a suitable answer," he replied. "It ain't suitable. That's what I've been seeing for the first time this morning. The point is—why was you interested in beetles, and why was I interested in bits o' string and stamps?"

"Yes, he's quite right," said Sarakoff; "that certainly is the point."

"To say that we are interested in a thing is no suitable explanation," continued the policeman. "After I'd done collecting stamps——"

"Why don't you arrest these two blokes?" shouted the taxi-man suddenly. "Why can't you do yer duty, you blue fathead?"

"I'm coming to that," said the policeman imperturbably. "As I was saying, after I collected stamps, I collected knives—any sort of old rusty knife—and then I joined the force and began to collect men, I collected all sorts o' men—tall and short, fat and thin. Now why did I do that?"

"It seems to me," observed the taxi-man, suddenly calm, "that somebody will be collecting you soon, and there won't be no need to arsk the reason why."

"That's where you and me don't agree," said the policeman. "I came to the conclusion this morning that we don't ask the reason why enough—not by 'alf. Now if somebody did as you say, and started collectin' policemen, what would be the reason?"

"Reason?" shouted the taxi-man. "Don't arsk me for a reason."

He turned to his taxi-cab and jerked the starting handle violently. The clatter of the engine arose. He climbed into his seat, and pulled at his gears savagely. In a few moments he had turned his cab, after wrenching in fury at the steering-wheel, and was jolting down the road in the morning brightness in search of breakfast.

CHAPTER XXVII

LEONORA'S VOICE

"My theory," said the policeman, "is that collectin'—and by that I mean all sorts of collection, including that of money—comes from a craving to 'ave something what other people 'aven't got. It comes from a kind o' pride which is foolish. Take a man like Morgan, for instance. Now he spent his life collecting dollars, and he never once stopped to ask 'imself why he was doin' it. I 'eard a friend of mine, a socialist he was, saying as 'ow no one had wasted his life more than Morgan. At the time it struck me as a silly kind of thing to say. But now I seem to see it in a different light." He meditated for some minutes. "It's the reason why—that's what we 'aven't thought of near enough."

I was about to reply when a motor-car stopped before us. It was a large green limousine. It drew up suddenly, with a scraping of tyres, and a woman got out of it. I recognized her at once. It was Leonora. She was wearing a motoring-coat of russet-brown material, and her hat was tied with a veil.

"Alexis!" she exclaimed.

Sarakoff roused himself. He stood up and bowed.

"What are you doing here?" she asked.

"Leonora," he said, "I am so glad to see you. We are just taking the air, and discussing a few matters of general interest." He patted her on the shoulder. "I congratulate you, Leonora. You are an Immortal. It suits you very well."

She was certainly one of the Immortals. The stain in her eyes was wonderfully vivid, but it did not produce a displeasing effect, as I had fancied it would. Indeed, her eyes had lost their hard restless look, and in place of it was an expression of bewilderment.

"What has happened to me?" she exclaimed. "Alexis, what is this that you have done to me?"

"What I told you about at the Pyramid Restaurant. You have got the germ in you and now you are immortal. Sit down, Leonora. I find it warmer when I am sitting. My friend and I had to leave Harley Street somewhat hurriedly, and I had not time to dress."

She sat down and loosened her veil.

"Last night a dreadful thing happened," she said. "And yet, although it was dreadful, I do not feel upset about it. I have been

115

trying to feel upset—as I should—but I can't. Let me tell you about it. I lay down yesterday afternoon in my room after tea to rest. I always do that when I can. I think I fell asleep for a moment. Then I felt a curious light feeling, as if I had suddenly been for a long holiday, and I got up. Alexis, when I saw myself in the glass I was horrified. I had the Blue Disease."

"Of course," said Sarakoff. "You were bound to get it. You knew that."

"I didn't know what to do. I wasn't very upset, only I felt something dreadful had happened. Well, I went to the Opera as usual and everyone was very sympathetic, but I said I was all right. But when my call came I suddenly knew—quite calmly, but certainly—that I could not sing properly. I went on the stage and began, but it was just as if I were singing for the first time in my life. They had to ring the curtain down. I apologized. I was quite calm and smiling. But there the fact remained—I had lost my voice. I had failed in public."

"Extraordinary," muttered Sarakoff. "Are you sure it was not just nervousness?"

"No, I'm certain of that. I felt absolutely self-possessed; far more so that I usually do, and that is saying a lot. No, my voice has gone. The Blue Disease has destroyed it. And yet I somehow don't feel any resentment. I don't understand. Richard, tell me what has happened."

I shook my head.

"I don't know," I said. "I can't explain. The germ is doing things that I never foresaw."

"I ought to be furious with you," she said.

"Try to be—if you can," smiled Sarakoff. "That's one of the strange things. I can't be furious. I have only two emotions—perfect calmness, or violent, horrible fear."

"Fear?" she exclaimed.

"Yes, fear of the worst kind conceivable."

"I understand the perfect calmness," she said, "but the fear— no."

"You will understand in time."

The policeman listened to our conversation with grave attention. Leonora was sitting between Sarakoff and me, and did not seem to find the presence of the visitor surprising. The green limousine stood in the road before us, the chauffeur sitting at the wheel looking steadily in front of him. The Heath seemed remarkably empty. The mist over London was lifting under the influence of the sun.

116

I was revolving in my mind a theory as to why Leonora had lost her voice. I already knew that the germ produced odd changes in the realm of likes and dislikes. I remembered Sarakoff's words that the germ was killing desire. My thoughts were clear, easy and lucid, and the problem afforded by Leonora's singular experience gave me a sense of quiet enjoyment. If the germ really did do away with desire, why should it at the same time do away with Leonora's wonderful voice? I recalled with marvellous facility everything I knew about her. My memory supplied me with every detail at the dinner of the PyramidRestaurant. The words of Sarakoff, which had at the time seemed coarse, came back to me. He had called her a vain ambitious cold-hearted woman, who thought that her voice and her beauty could not be beaten.

My reflections were interrupted by the policeman.

"The lady," he remarked, "has lost her voice sudden-like. Now I lost my 'abit of arresting people sudden-like too. I lost it this morning. Any other time I should have taken the gentleman in the dressing-gown in charge for being improperly dressed. But this morning it don't come natural to me. If he wants to wear a dressing-gown on the Spaniard's Walk, he presumably 'as his own reasons. It don't concern me."

"It seems to me that the germ takes ambition out of us," said Sarakoff.

"Ambition?" said the policeman. "No, that ain't right. I've got ambition still—only it's a different kind of ambition."

"I have no ambition now," said Leonora at length. "Alexis is right. This malady has taken the ambition out of me. I may be Immortal, but if I am, then I am an Immortal without ambition. I seem to be lost, to be suddenly diffused into space or time, to be a kind of vapour. Something has dissolved in me—something hard, bright, alert. I do not know why I am here. The car came round as usual to take me for my morning run. I got in—why I don't know."

Sarakoff was studying her attentively.

"It is very strange," he said. "You used to arouse a feeling of strength and determination in me, Leonora. You used to stimulate me intensely. This morning I only feel one thing about you."

"What is that?"

"I feel that I have cheated you."

"Cheated her?" exclaimed the policeman. "How do you come to that conclusion?"

"I've destroyed the one thing that was herself—I've destroyed desire in her. I've left her a mind devoid of all values tacked on to a body that no longer interests her. For what was Leonora, who filled the hearts of men with madness, but an incarnation of desire?"

117

CHAPTER XXVIII

THE KILLING OF DESIRE

We drove in Leonora's car through London. The streets were crowded. I do not think that much routine work was done that day. People formed little crowds on the pavements, and at Oxford Circus someone was speaking to a large concourse from the seat of a motor lorry.

Leonora seemed extraordinarily apathetic. She leaned back in the car and seemed uninterested in the passing scene. Sarakoff, wrapped up in a fur rug, stared dreamily in front of him. As far as I can recall them, my feelings during that swift tour of London were vague. The buildings, the people, the familiar signs in the streets, the shop windows, all seemed to have lost in some degree the quality of reality. I was detached from them; and whenever I made an effort to rouse myself, the ugliness and meaninglessness of everything I saw seemed strangely emphasized.

When we reached Harley Street we found my house little damaged, save for a broken panel in the green front door and a few panes of glass smashed in the lower windows. The house was empty. The servants had vanished.

Leonora said she wished to go home and she drove off in the car. Sarakoff did not even wave farewell to her, but went straight up to his room and lay down on the bed. I went into the study and sat in my chair by the fireplace.

I was roused by the opening of the door, and looking up I saw a face that I recognized, but for the moment I could not fit a name to it. My visitor came in calmly, and sat down opposite me.

"My name is Thornduck," he said. "I came to consult you about my health a few days ago."

"I remember," I said.

"Your front door was open so I walked in."

I nodded. His eyes, stained with blue, rested on me.

"I have been thinking," he said. "It struck me that there was something you forgot to tell me the other day."

I nodded again.

"You began, if you remember, by asking me if I believed in miracles. That set me thinking, and as I saw your name in the paper,

118

connected with the Blue Disease, I knew you were a miracle-monger. How did you do it?"

"I don't know. It was all due to my black cat. Tripped over it, got concussion and regained my senses with the idea that led up to the germ."

He smiled.

"A black cat," he mused. "I wonder if it's all black magic?"

"That's what Hammer suggested. I don't know what kind of magic it is."

"Of course it is magic," said Thornduck.

"Magic?"

"Of course. Have you even thought what kind of magic it is?"

"No."

"A big magic, such as you have worked, is just bringing the distant future into the present with a rush."

"Sarakoff had some such idea," I murmured. "He spoke of anticipating our evolution by centuries at one stroke."

"Exactly. That's magic. The question remains—is it black magic?" He crossed his thin legs and leaned back in the chair. "I got the Blue Disease the day before yesterday and since then I've thought more than I have ever done in all my life. When I read in the paper this morning that you said the Blue Disease conferred immortality on people I was not surprised. I had come to the same conclusion in a roundabout way. But I want to ask you one question. Did you know beforehand that it killed desire?"

"No. Neither Sarakoff nor I foresaw that."

"Well, if you had let me into your confidence before I could have told you that right away in the general principle contained in the saying that you can't eat your cake and have it. It's just another aspect of the law of the conservation of energy, isn't it?"

"I always had a doubt——"

"Naturally. It's intuitional. The laws of the universe are just intuitions put into words. You've carried out an enormous spiritual experiment to prove what all religions have always asserted however obscurely. All religion teaches that you can't eat your cake and have it. That's the essence of religion, and you, formerly a cut-and-dried scientist, have gone and proved it to the whole world for eternity. Rather odd, isn't it?"

I watched his face with interest. It was thin and the complexion was transparent. His eyes, wonderfully wide and brilliantly stained by the germ, produced in me a new sensation. It was akin to enthusiasm, but in it was something of love, such as I had never experienced for any man. I became uplifted. My whole

119

being began to vibrate to some strangely delicate and exquisite influence, and I knew that Thornduck was the medium through which these impulses reached me. It was not his words but the atmosphere round him that raised me temporarily to this degree of receptivity.

"It is odd," I said.

He continued to look at me.

"You have a message for me?" I observed at last.

"Why, yes, I have," he replied. "You have done wrong, Harden. You have worked black magic, and it will fail out of sheer necessity."

"Tell me what I have done."

"You have artificially produced a condition of life many ages before humanity is ready to receive it. The body of desire is being worked up by endless labour into something more delicate and sensitive—into a transmutation that we can only dimly understand. At present the whole plot of life is based on the principle of desire and in this way people are kept busy, constantly spurred on to thought and activity by essentially selfish motives. It is only in abstract thought that the selfless ideal has a real place as yet, but the very fact that it is there shows what lies at the top of the ladder that humanity is so painfully climbing. As long as desire is the plot of life, death is necessary, for its terrible shadow sharpens desire and makes the prizes more alluring and the struggle more desperate. And so man goes on, ceaselessly active and striving, for without activity and striving there is no perfecting of the instrument. You can't have upward progress in conditions of stagnation. All that strange incredible side of life, called the Devil, is the inner plot of life that makes the wheels go round and evolution possible. It is vitally necessary to keep the vast machinery running at the present level of evolution. Desire is the furnace in the engine-house. The wheels go round and the fabric is slowly and intricately spun and only pessimists and bigots fail to see evidence of any purpose in it all. Now what has your Blue Disease done? It has taken the whole plot out of life at its present stage of development at one fell swoop. It has killed Desire—put out the furnace before the pattern in the fabric is nearly complete."

"But I never could see that, Thornduck. How could I foresee that?"

"If you had had a grain of vision you would have known that you couldn't give humanity the gift of immortality without some compensatory loss. The law of compensation is as sure as the law of gravity—you ought to know that."

"I had dim feelings—I knew Sarakoff was wrong, with his

120

dream of physical bliss—but how could I foresee that desire would go?"

"As a mere scientist, test-tube in hand, you couldn't. But you're better than that. You've got a glimmering of moral imagination in you."

He fell into a reverie.

"You are keeping something back. Tell me plainly what you mean," I asked.

"Don't you see that if the germ lasts any length of time," he said, "the machinery will run down and—stop?"

CHAPTER XXIX

THE REVOLT OF THE YOUNG

Amid all the strife and clamour of the next few days one thing stands out now in my mind with sinister radiance. It is that peculiar form of lawlessness which broke out and had as its object the destruction of the old.

There is no doubt that the idea of immortality got hold of people and carried them away completely. The daily miracles that were occurring of the renewal of health and vigour, the cure of disease and the passing of those infirmities that are associated with advancing years, impressed the popular imagination deeply. As a result there grew up a widespread discontent and bitterness. The young—those who were as yet free from the germ—conceived in their hearts that an immense injustice had been done to them.

It must be remembered that life at that time had taken on a strange and abnormal aspect. Its horizons had been suddenly altered by the germ. Although breadth had been given to it from the point of years, a curious contraction had appeared at the same time. It was a contraction felt most acutely by those in inferior positions. It was a contraction that owed its existence to the sense of being shut in eternally by those in higher positions, whom death no longer would remove at convenient intervals. The student felt it as he looked at his professor. The clerk felt it as he looked at his manager. The subaltern felt it as he looked at his colonel. The daughter felt it when she looked at her mother, and the son when he looked at his father. The germ had given simultaneously a tremendous blow to freedom, and a tremendous impetus to freedom.

Thus, perhaps for the first time in history, there swiftly began an accumulation and concentration of those forces of discontent which, in normal times, only manifest themselves here and there in the relationships between old and young men, and are regarded with good-humoured patience. A kind of war broke out all over the country.

This war was terrible in its nature. All the secret weariness and unspoken bitterness of the younger generation found a sudden outlet. Goaded to madness by the prospect of a future of continual repression, in which the old would exercise an undiminished authority, the younger men and women plunged into a form of

122

excess over which a veil must be drawn.... There is only one thing which can be recorded in their favour. Chloroform and drowning appear to have been the methods most often used, and they are perhaps merciful ways of death. The great London clubs became sepulchres. All people who had received the highest distinctions and honours, whose names were household words, were removed with ruthless determination. Scarcely a single well-known man or woman of the older generation, whose name was honoured in science, literature, art, business or politics, was spared. All aged and wealthy people perished. A clean sweep was made, and made with a decision and unanimity that was incredible.

It is painful now to recall the terrible nature of that civil war. It lasted only a short time, but it opened my eyes to the inner plan upon which mortal man is based. For I am compelled to admit that this widespread murder, that suddenly flashed into being, was founded upon impulses that lie deep in man's heart. They were those giant impulses that lie behind growth, and the effect of the germ was merely to throw them suddenly into the broad light of day, unchained, grim and implacable.

Fortunately, the germ spread steadily and quickly, killing as it did so all hate and desire.

Jason, still free from the germ, flung himself into the general uproar with extraordinary vigour. It was clear that he thought the great opportunity had come which would eventually bring him to the height of his power. To check the growing lawlessness and murder he advocated a new adjustment of property. Big meetings were held in the public spaces of London, and some wild ideas were formulated.

In the meantime the medical profession, as far as the men yet free from the germ were concerned, continued its work in a dull, mechanical way. Each day the number of patients fell lower, as the Blue Disease slowly spread. Hammer, himself an Immortal, came to see me once, but only to speak of the necessity for the immediate simplification of houses. It was odd to observe how, once a man became infected, his former interests and anxieties fell away from him like an old garment. In Harley Street an attitude of stubborn disbelief continued amongst those still mortal. There is something magnificent in that adamantine spirit which refuses to recognize the new, even though it moves with ever-increasing distinctness before the very eyes of the deniers. I was not surprised. I was familiar with medical men.

Meanwhile the Royal Family became infected by the germ, and passed out of the public eye. The Prime Minister became a victim and vanished. For once a man had the germ in his system, as far as externals were concerned, he almost ceased to exist.

The infection of Jason occurred in my presence. He had come in to explain to me a proposed line of campaign as regards the marriage laws.

"This germ of yours has given people the courage to think!" he exclaimed. "It is extraordinary how timid people were in thinking. It has launched them out, and now is the time to bring in new proposals."

"In all your calculations, you omit to recollect the effects of the germ," I said. "Surely you have seen by now that it changes human nature totally?"

He stared at me uncomprehendingly. He was one of those men, so common in public life, who have no power of understanding what they themselves have not experienced. He continued with undiminished enthusiasm.

"We must have marriage contracts for definite periods. With the increased state of health, and the full span of life confronting every man, we must face the problem squarely. Now what stands in our way?"

He got up and went to the window. It was a dull foggy day, and there was frost on the ground. He stared outside for some moments.

"What, I repeat, stands in our way?"

"Well?"

"The Church, and a mass of superstitions that we have inherited from the Old Testament. That's what stands in our way. We still attach more value to the Old Testament than to the New. The Scotch, for example, like the Jews.... Yes, of course.... What was I saying?"

He left the window and sat down once more before me, moving rather listlessly.

"Yes, Harden. Of course. That's what it is, isn't it? Do you remember—diddle—yes it was diddle, diddle——"

He paused and frowned.

"Hey diddle diddle, the cat and the fiddle," he muttered, "Yes—hey, diddle, diddle, diddle—that's what it is, isn't it?"

"Of course," I said. "It's all really that."

"Just diddle, diddle, diddle?"

"Yes—if you like."

"That is substituting diddle for riddle," he said earnestly. He frowned again and passed his hand across his eyes.

"Yes," I said calmly. "It's going a step up."

I suppose about half an hour passed before either of us spoke again after this extraordinary termination to our conversation. In absolute silence we sat facing one another and during that time I saw the blue stain growing clearer and clearer in Jason's eyes. At last he rose.

"It's very odd," he said. "Tell me, were you like this?"

"How do you feel?"

"As if I had been drunk and suddenly had been made sober. I will leave you. I want to think. I will go down to the country."

"And your papers?"

"We must have a new Press," he said, and left the room.

That same day the great railway accident occurred just outside London that led to the death of sixty people, many of them Immortals. Its effect on public imagination was profound. All dangerous enterprises became invested with a terrible radiance. Men asked themselves if, in face of a future of health, it was worth risking life in rashness of any description, and gradually traffic came to a standstill. Long before the germ had infected the whole populace all activities fraught with danger had ceased. The coal mines were abandoned. The railways were silent. The streets of London became empty of traffic.

Blue-stained people began to throng the streets of London in vast masses, moving to and fro without aim or purpose, perfectly orderly, vacant, lost—like Sarakoff's butterflies....

Thornduck came to see me one day when the reign of the germ was practically absolute in London.

"They are wandering into the country in thousands," he remarked. "They have lost all sense of home and possession. They are vague, trying to form an ideal socialistic community. What a mess your germ is making of life! They're not ready for it. The question is whether they will rouse themselves to consider the food question."

"We need scarcely any food," I replied. "I've had nothing to eat to-day."

"Nor I. But since we're still linked up to physical bodies we must require some nourishment."

"I have eaten two biscuits and a little cheese in the last twenty-four hours. Surely you don't think that food is to be a serious problem under such circumstances?"

"It might be. You must remember that initiative is now destroyed in the vast majority of people. They may permit themselves to die of inanition. Can you say you have an appetite now?"

125

I reflected for some time, striving to recall the feeling of hunger that belonged to the days of desire.

"No. I have no appetite."

"Think carefully. In place of appetite have you no tendencies?"

"I feel a kind of lethargy," I said at last. "I felt it yesterday and to-day it is stronger."

"As if you wished to sleep?"

"Not exactly. But it is akin to that. I have some difficulty in keeping my attention on things. There is a kind of pull within me away from—away from reality."

He nodded.

"I went in to see your Russian friend. He's upstairs. He is not exactly asleep. He is more like a man partially under the influence of a drug."

"I will go and see him," I said.

Sarakoff was lying on the bed with his eyes shut. He was breathing quietly. His eyelids quivered, as if they might open at any moment, but my entrance did not rouse him. His limbs were relaxed. I spoke to him and tried to wake him, without result. Then I remembered how I had stumbled across the body of Herbert Wain in the Park some days ago. He had seemed to be in a strange kind of sleep. I sat down on the bed and stared at the motionless figure of the Russian. There was something strangely pathetic in his pose. His rough hair and black beard, his keen aquiline face seemed weirdly out of keeping with his helpless state. Here lay the man whose brain had once teemed with ambitious desires, relaxed and limp like a baby, while the nails of his hands, turquoise blue, bore silent witness to his great experiment on humanity. Had it failed? Where was all that marvellous vision of physical happiness that had haunted him? The streets of London were filled with people, no longer working, no longer crying or weeping, but moving aimlessly, like people in a dream. Were they happy? I moved to the window and drew down the blind.

"This may be the end," I thought. "The germ will be sweeping through France now. It may be the end of all things."

I rejoined Thornduck in the study.

"Sarakoff is in a kind of trance," I observed. "What do you make of it?"

"Isn't it natural?" he asked. "What kind of a man was he? What motives did he work on? Just think what the killing of desire means. All those things that depended on worldly ambition, self-gratification, physical pleasure, conceit, lust, hatred, passion, egotism, selfishness, vanity, avarice, sensuality and so on, are

126

undermined and rendered paralysed by the germ. What remains? Why, in most people, practically nothing remains."

"Even so," I said, "I don't see why Sarakoff should go into a trance."

"He's gone into a trance simply because there's not enough left in him to constitute an individuality. The germ has taken the inside clean out of him. He's just an immortal shell now."

"Then do you think——?"

I stared at him wonderingly.

"I think that the germ will send most of the world to sleep."

He got up and walked to the window. The clear noonday light fell on his thin sensitive face and accentuated the pallor of his skin.

"All those who are bound on the wheel of desire will fall asleep," he murmured. A smile flickered on his lips and he turned and looked at me.

"Harden," he said, "it's really very funny. It's infinitely humorous, isn't it?"

"I see nothing humorous in anything," I replied. "I've lost all sense of humour."

He raised his eyebrows.

"Of humour?" he queried. "Surely not. Humour is surely immortal."

CHAPTER XXX

THE GREAT SLEEP

On that day the animals in London fell asleep with few exceptions. The exceptions were, I believe, all dogs. I do not pretend to explain, how it came about that dogs remained awake longer than other animals. The reason may be that dogs have some quality in them which is superior even to the qualities found in man, for there is a sweetness in the nature of dogs that is rare in men and women.

Many horses were overcome in the streets and lay down where they were. No attempt was made to remove them. They were left, stretched out on their sides, apparently unconscious.

And many thousands of men and women fell asleep. In some cases men were overcome by the sleep before their dogs, which has always seemed strange to me. It was Thornduck who told me this, for he remained awake during this period that the germ reigned supreme. He tells me that I fell asleep the next evening in my chair in the study and that he carried me upstairs to my room. I had just returned from visiting Leonora, whom I had found unconscious. He made a tour of London next morning. In the City there was a profound stillness.

In the West End matters were much the same. In Cavendish Square he entered many houses and found silence and sleep within. Everywhere doors and windows were wide open, giving access to any who might desire it. He visited the Houses of Parliament only to find a few comatose blue-stained men lying about on the benches. For the sleep had overtaken people by stealth. One day, passing by the Zoo, he had climbed the fence and made an inspection of the inmates. With the exception of an elephant that was nodding drowsily, the animals lay motionless in their cages, deep in the trance that the germ induced.

From time to time he met a man or woman awake like himself and stopped to talk. Those who still retained sufficient individuality to continue existence were the strangest mixture of folk, for they were of every class, many of them being little better than beggars. They were people in whom the desire of life played a minor part. They were those people who are commonly regarded as being failures, people who live and die unknown to the world. They were those people who devote themselves to an obscure existence, shun the rewards of successful careers, and are ridiculed by all prosperous individuals. It seems that Thornduck was instrumental in calling a meeting of these people at St. Paul's. There were about two thousand of them in all, but many in the outlying suburbs remained ignorant of the meeting, and Thornduck considers that in the London district alone there must have been some thousands who did not attend. At the meeting, which must have been the strangest in all history, the question of the future was discussed. Many believed that the effect of the germ on those in the great sleep would ultimately lead to a cessation of life owing to starvation. Thornduck held that the germ would pass, arguing on principles that were so unscientific that I refrain from giving them. Eventually it appears that a decision was reached to leave London on a certain date and migrate southwards in search of a region where a colony might be founded under laws and customs suitable for Immortals. Thornduck says that there was one thing that struck him very forcibly at the meeting at St. Paul's. All the people gathered there had about them a certain sweetness and strength, which, although it was very noticeable, escaped his powers of analysis.

He attempted on several occasions to get into telegraphic communication with the Continent, but failed. In his wanderings he entered many homes, always being careful to lay out at full length any of the unconscious inmates who were asleep on chairs, for he feared that they might come to harm, and that their limbs might become stiffened into unnatural postures.

All the time he had a firm conviction that the phase of sleep was temporary. He himself had moments in which a slight drowsiness overtook him, but he never lost the enhanced power of thought that I had experienced in the early stages of the Blue Disease. So absolute was his conviction that a general awakening would come about that he began to busy his mind with the question as to what he could do, in conjunction with the other Immortals who were still awake, to benefit humanity when it should emerge from the trance. This question was discussed continually. Many thought that they should burn all records, financial, political, governmental and private, so that some opportunity of starting afresh might be given to mankind, enslaved to the past and fettered by law and custom. But the danger of chaos resulting from such a step deterred him. He confessed that the more he thought on the subject the more clearly he saw that under the circumstances belonging to its stage of evolution, the organization of the world was suited to the race that inhabited it. All change, he saw, had to come from within, and that to alter external conditions suddenly and artificially might do incredible harm. We were constructed to develop against resistance, and to remove such resistances before they had been overcome naturally was to tamper with the inner laws of life. And so, after long discussion, they did nothing....

It is curious to reflect that they, earnest men devoted to progress, having at their mercy the machinery of existence, walked through the midst of sleeping London and did nothing. But then none of them were fanatics, for Thornduck stated that the fanatics fell early to sleep, thus proving that the motives behind their fanaticism were egotistical, and a source of satisfaction to themselves. He made a point of visiting the homes of some of them. Philanthropists, too, succumbed early.

On the seventh day after the great sleep had overtaken London the effects of the germ began to wane. Those who had fallen asleep latest were the earliest to open their eyes. The blue stain rapidly vanished from eyes, skin and nails.... I regained my waking sense on the evening of the seventh day and found myself in a small country cottage whither Thornduck had borne me in a motor-car, fearing lest awakened London might seek some revenge on the discoverers of the germ. Sarakoff lay on a couch beside me, still fast asleep.

The first clear idea that came to me concerned Alice Annot. I determined to go to her at once. Then I remembered with vexation that I had wantonly smashed two vases worth ten pounds apiece.

I struggled to my feet. My hands were thin and wasted. I was ravenous with hunger. I felt giddy.

"What's the time?" I called confusedly. "It must be very late. Wake up!"

And I stooped down and began to shake Sarakoff violently.

THE END